THE STATE WE'RE IN

Maine Stories

ANN BEATTIE

SCRIBNER

New York   London   Toronto   Sydney   New Delhi

SCRIBNER
An Imprint of Simon & Schuster, Inc.
1230 Avenue of the Americas
New York, NY 10020

Copyright © 2015 by Ann Beattie

All rights reserved, including the right to reproduce this book
or portions thereof in any form whatsoever. For information, address
Scribner Subsidiary Rights Department,
1230 Avenue of the Americas, New York, NY 10020.

First Scribner hardcover edition August 2015

SCRIBNER and design are registered trademarks of The Gale Group, Inc.,
used under license by Simon & Schuster, Inc., the publisher of this work.

For information about special discounts for bulk purchases,
please contact Simon & Schuster Special Sales at 1-866-506-1949
or business@simonandschuster.com.

The Simon & Schuster Speakers Bureau can bring authors to
your live event. For more information or to book an event,
contact the Simon & Schuster Speakers Bureau at 1-866-248-3049
or visit our website at www.simonspeakers.com.

Interior design by Kyle Kabel

Manufactured in the United States of America

1 3 5 7 9 10 8 6 4 2

Library of Congress Cataloging-in-Publication Data is available.

ISBN 978-1-5011-0781-8
ISBN 978-1-5011-0782-5 (ebook)

"Lying in a Hammock at William Duffy's Farm in Pine Island, Minnesota"
in *The Branch Will Not Break* by James Wright © 1963
Published by Wesleyan University Press and used by permission.

For Charles and Holly Wright

CONTENTS

CONTENTS

THE STATE
WE'RE IN

WHAT MAGICAL
REALISM WOULD BE

The summer school assignment, the fucking fucking summer school third paper of ten, and if you didn't get at least a C on the first nine, you had to write eleven papers, the fucking teacher wadding up her big fat lips so they looked like a carnation, her lips that she'd use to pout at your inadequacy . . . this paper, to hold their interest, was supposed to be about Magical Realism, and although you didn't have to read all of the Márquez book the teacher soooooooo loved, she had distributed several paragraphs from the book in which weird things happened, and your paper was supposed to go on forever, like the writer, then have the clouds howl, or something. "Not a metaphor! Or, not merely to be thought of metaphorically!" she'd exclaimed. "The psychological state has to matter. You have to embody emotion in the stretch you make." She gestured with her gangly arms. The woman was at least six feet tall, every bit as tall as Jocelyn's uncle. Writing essays was retarded. It completely was. Summer with her aunt and uncle was torture, from start to the yet-to-come finish, which would end when the days were no longer long and when the flowers began to droop and the water was totally too cold to swim in at the York Harbor beach, where summer brides who were way too old to get married came out onto the lawn and stuff blew all around them, their veils, their hair, their bouquets, everything airborne. One bride sprained her ankle running after her stupid pink lilies and baby's breath—she went down like Humpty Dumpty and a seagull swooped up the bouquet and dropped it, but too far out over the rocks for anybody to retrieve it, although the best man tried. But that—real life—you couldn't write. You had to write Magical Realism, in which no doubt the seagull could recite Latin proverbs while it was being philosophical about the flowers not being fish.

Now was the hour: Uncle Raleigh would look at what she'd written and offer advice and encouragement, while she mentally corkscrewed her finger outside her ear and pitied him because he had no job, and he limped, and he was a nice man, but also sort of an idiot. In any case, he—her mother's brother—was a lot nicer than his dim wife, Aunt Bettina Louise Tompkins, whose initials were BLT. Hold the mayo.

"Lovely evening on the porch. Sorry you couldn't join us, but what you're doing is more important," Uncle Raleigh said. "You know, you have an intelligent expression, you've got those expressive eyes of your mother's. I never doubted your intelligence for a second, from the day you were born. You do have all my sympathy for not being able to be with your friends this summer, but you'll show 'em all, including

Bettina, who's been on your case for nothing, I know. You want to cornrow your hair, what of it? Not like you're coming home with 'Satan' tattooed on the back of your hand."

"I'm afraid of needles. Thanks for saying something nice to me."

"That's because I believe you deserve niceness, Jocelyn. Well—Bettina's insisting I scan your essay, so if you don't mind, could you print it out, because I can't read that little screen, as you know. And as I tell you every single night."

She got up from his office chair, where she'd been slumped, writing and picking at her pedicure. She turned on his printer. When it printed out, it was not quite two pages.

"Yesterday's was three pages," he said immediately.

"She's tired of reading long papers." Jocelyn lied to Raleigh and Bettina—certainly to Bettina—and to her sort of best friend, who was lucky enough to be in Australia this summer, even if it did have to be with her family and her retarded—really, actually retarded—brother, the *challenged* Daniel Junior, who picked his nose right in front of you.

"Looks good to me," Raleigh said, nodding in agreement with himself. "You see that colon, though. I thought that was the punctuation mark when you're going to have a whole list of things, and you've only got one, so maybe you could say, 'Such as a turtle' rather than 'Such as: turtle.'"

She made the correction. His bad leg was the result of a motorcycle accident when he was in his twenties, not much older than she was now. At least somebody in her family had done *something*.

"Can I borrow the car tonight for an hour? Some kids from the summer program are getting together down at the beach at low tide. There's no drugs, alcohol, or sex. We're all too depressed to bother."

"I don't see why not, though Bettina certainly will," he said. "I'll tell her once I hear the ignition start. Remember, though: an intermediate license means none of your friends can be in the car. A word to the wise is that I'd head out of the driveway pretty fast."

He was scanning the second page of the essay (damn!). "Well, it gets a little drifty in the last paragraph, which is supposed to sum up what you've said before, isn't it?"

"No. There's new thinking about that now. You don't repeat yourself."

"I see. But it's not grammatically correct to say, 'Desideratum were what this field of flowers was.' I don't even really know what that big word means." He looked at her. "Not nasturtiums, you don't mean?"

"The purply flowers everywhere," she said. She was holding his keys now.

"Lupine," he said. "Loves to grow wild, but you get it into your garden, most of the time it won't take. It keeps to itself and that's how it prospers. A metaphor, to your teacher's way of thinking. I shouldn't make fun of her. I never knew so much until this summer."

"I'll change it when I get home. I promise."

"Fine, then. But tell me, what exactly does that big word mean?"

"It means, 'Go placidly amid the noise and haste,'" Bettina said. She was standing in the doorway, wearing her apron with the chicken head on it. She had two years of college and had worked for city government. She had about as much fashion sense as Jocelyn's mother, which began and ended with an underwire bra. Both of them were quite overweight. Jocelyn and Uncle Raleigh weren't, which gave them at least something in common beyond the fact that both of them were trapped in the house, except for his stupid golf night.

"So you got the keys to the car, you be careful. Only people with beach parking stickers can park on the paved road, I'm sure you know that. I don't want to pay any fifty-dollar fine," BLT said. "Raleigh okayed your essay?"

"He loved it," she said. He smiled benignly at his wife. He didn't look in her direction.

"On the way home maybe you could pick up a pizza at River Bend," she said. "They're open in the summer until ten, and I can phone it in at nine thirty. I don't feel like ice cream, I feel like a small regular pizza," she said. She'd had a cancer scare at Christmas. Since then, she'd gained considerable weight and often made announcements about what she wanted. Among these things was Neutrogena soap at *midnight*, so all she could do was have Jocelyn order it for her from Amazon Prime. Which her mother had already made clear she was not going to subscribe to anymore, once they raised their rates. That would last about a week. Her mother even relied on Amazon for crackers.

"You know," Raleigh said at the front door, "sometimes, to my way of thinking, big words just stick out and they're like a red flag in front of a bull. There might be a much simpler, straightforward way of concluding. Something to think about when you get home."

"That's a good idea," she said.

"What your aunt was talking about with that definition, I

don't know," he said. "I guess I'll check the dictionary. The real one, not Google, like the one you find things on in five seconds."

"You can even spell it all screwed up and it corrects it and you just click on the correction."

"I'm not going to say anything that will make me sound old. I'd be depressed like you young people, then. Best not to verbalize every feeling."

"Don't you want to get out of this place sometimes?" she said, twisting the loose part of her hair she'd dyed pink the same day she cut bangs.

"I have a secret life. I've broken almost every commandment," Raleigh said. "As your mother will be the first to tell you. Thing is, I've run out of steam."

"You don't get to admit that if you're my age," she said over her shoulder on her way down the steps. He turned on the porch light for her, though it wasn't dark yet. Now they were on the downside of the longest day of the year. Soon the days would be like riding a roller coaster. She'd taken one of Raleigh's Tylenol 2s once and given it to T. G., the cutest boy, whose taste ran more to simple things, like Red Bull and vodka to wash down a few antihistamines. He was really peculiar. Still, he'd appreciated the gesture. She wouldn't dare steal another. Bettina probably had hidden cameras in the house, she was so possessive. It was totally awesome that Becca had gotten to go to Australia and even went out on a boat to the Great Barrier Reef, which her father had dived into. While everyone waited for him to surface, Becca had thrown up in a bag. Jocelyn had no update, because her mother was totally opposed to her texting on vacation and had turned off the messaging on Jocelyn's phone.

Down at the beach, only the pretty girl, Angie, and her constant companion, Zelda, were standing where the water met the sand, Zelda with one of those dramatic Indian scarves her mother bought blowing from her neck like someone asking to be hanged. It was white with some sparkly things sewn on, she saw, as she came closer. "Hey," she said.

"Hey," Angie said. One of her strategies was to pretend she wasn't extremely pretty and that she was happy to see other girls. She was the same whether or not boys were around.

"Cool scarf," Jocelyn said. "How many of those do you have, Zelda?"

"They're mostly my mother's. She like hates to actually give one away so I just borrow them all the time. I'm tired of all of them. I don't wear blue anymore, anyway."

"It is so boring in that house," Jocelyn said, stepping out of her flip-flops, tossing them behind her on the sand. "I'm sure they haven't had sex for forty years. My mom told me Bettina almost went into a convent when she was a teenager. I don't know how he stands being there. He says he's tired."

"Me, too," Zelda said. "I slept five hours last night. I am completely living for the last day of class. I don't care if I never go to college, all I want to do is get out of this town any way I can, waitress, stripper, like I care. My mother's writing this person she knows at Yale, like Yale takes losers who get C pluses on their essays. Makes sense to me."

"You scored genius on your math SAT," Angie said. "Eight

hundred. Fucking eight hundred! Nobody does that. My brother's a biologist, and he scored seven hundred forty or something."

"Big deal," Zelda said. "I got another C on my last English essay."

"I don't think you were meant for English, I think you were meant for math," Angie said.

"Sure. Maybe I can teach it at Yale."

"You are so down on Yale!" Jocelyn said. "Do you realize how many times you bring it up?"

Zelda shrugged. The scarf blew across her face and probably got some pink lipstick on it. She didn't really try to keep up with Angie, but most nights she applied one thing: one night mascara, another night lipstick.

"So what did you write about?" Angie said, her eyes downcast. "I can't even believe this is what we have to talk to each other about. I guess we could just shut up and not say anything."

"I thought T. G. was coming down tonight," Jocelyn said.

"Tell her," Angie said to Zelda.

"What? Like you can't? He's in the ER getting his stomach pumped. He texted me. He put down a bottle of Ambien, or something, and barfed it all up on Stoli. The dog was licking his face when his father walked in."

"No way," Jocelyn said.

"Your *booooooooy*friend," Zelda said. "Or at least, one of the few guys in the class who isn't a sociopath, or something. That kid that cuts himself? Way gross! All that blood getting flicked around under the desk. We could get AIDS."

"The ER," Jocelyn echoed. "Wow."

"He'll text when he's out." Zelda shrugged.

"Should we visit him, or something?" Angie said suddenly.

"They don't let friends visit each other in the ER," Jocelyn said.

"Well, I would," Zelda said. "It would be good for morale."

"That's the Army or something," Angie said. "Mo-raaaale," she drawled.

The stars were out over the water. Jocelyn thought the slight heavy feeling in her stomach might be because she was about to get her period. Her mother had had a hysterectomy. It was one of the reasons she'd sent Jocelyn to her aunt and uncle's. She felt so weak and sick. And Bettina had made such a pitch for the "accelerated" summer program. What did that mean? Like you never put on the brake? If she could, she'd pull up a hand brake. Just WHAM! and even with the seat belt she'd be nose to nose with the windshield, the car would stop so suddenly.

"I wrote about Lupine," she said. "I couldn't get the Magical Realism part about them, though. I'm also so retarded, I got the wrong word, but my uncle knew what flowers I meant. I think I'm going to figure out a way the whole field can lift up and become the sky, or something."

"It gets Raptured?" Zelda said.

"And it would turn out that we're really walking in the sky and then there's this flash of Earth, and then the planet revolves, or something. I mean, she'd go with anything, if the grammar was correct."

Zelda laughed. Jocelyn noticed that she'd painted her toes pale green.

"When I was little, my parents had a sleeping porch. We'd

all three of us be out there in July and most of August. Then my father closed it in," Angie said.

"My mother's worried about losing our house. She says she's getting a reverse mortgage, but Uncle Raleigh says she is not. He's trying to find a job. He quit the other one because he had to stand up all day, but now he wishes he hadn't."

"What age are those people?" Angie asked.

"He's like ten years older than my mother. He's sixty."

"Sixty. I can't even imagine my parents at sixty. They had me when they were twenty, so they're thirty-six. Sixty!" Angie said. "I guess people live longer now."

"That's Cassiopeia," Zelda said, twining her scarf around her throat, then tugging it down. "Why wouldn't the Big Dipper be out?"

"It's too depressed. It's at home, writing an essay: 'My Life as the Big Dipper,'" Jocelyn said. "I've got to fix the end of my essay. I said I'd be back in an hour. That gives me how much time before I have to go?"

Zelda checked her cell phone. "Twenty-five minutes, more or less," she said. "I didn't notice exactly when you came."

Jocelyn thought she might just drive past the hospital. She could go in and ask if he was okay, even if they wouldn't tell her anything. When her own mother was hospitalized, they wouldn't tell her anything. They'd only tell Bettina. And Raleigh, too, though he was never at the hospital because he had an anxiety thing if he walked into one. He had to carry smelling salts in sealed packets, like substitute sugar. She and Raleigh had gone to matinees—he was pretty great about that; he'd watch anything—and they'd eaten wherever she wanted, so she'd ordered a lot of really fresh, tasty stuff at Chipotle, and then they'd bought takeout for BLT, which always leaked out of the container, though neither Raleigh nor she could ever figure out how that happened every time.

"My parents were married on the beach in Nantucket," Angie said. "There was a string quartet, with my cousin playing cello and worried all the time about sand blowing into it, apparently. I was inside Mom. I was attending as a fetus."

"I never want to get married," Zelda said. "Quote me on that if I say I'm engaged."

"I will," Angie said. "I think we should both skip the whole marriage thing and hope we turn into lesbians."

"Ugh," Zelda said.

"Maybe I'll give Uncle Raleigh a break and head back early," Jocelyn said. "He's really been supernice to me, especially considering how oppressed he is."

"Maybe you can marry us before you go. People do it with just some certificate they get over the Internet, anyway." Angie grabbed Zelda's hand. Zelda pulled her hand back. "Say, 'I marry you, I hereby marry you. You are now married,'" she said.

"What is that country where you can say, 'I divorce you, I divorce you, I divorce you' and it's true?" Jocelyn said.

"You made that up," Angie said.

"No, really. It's true."

"Because NPR said it, or something?" Zelda said, taking Angie's hand. "Oh, darling, NPR says we're divorced!" she said.

Jocelyn laughed and toed a little wet sand toward them. It was their ritual: they'd send some wet sand in the other's direction, sand like instantly appearing wrinkles, or like a pug

11

dog's scruff. Angie's mother had two pugs. They snorted all night and kept everyone awake. Angie could do a very funny imitation of everyone: her distraught mother, talking to the dogs; her father, throwing them out in the middle of the night; the pugs, snorting.

"Okay, well, you ace it with your story about flowers in the sky, your 'Lucy in the Sky with Diamonds' story," Zelda said. She hated for people to go. She always said something to keep them. She toed another bit of wet sand in Jocelyn's direction. It looked like shit. That was what it looked like, wet and more brown than gray.

She drove through the parking lot of the hospital, but didn't go in. She turned on the radio and heard that rain and thunder were predicted later, and also the next day. Maybe it would rain out her uncle's golf game.

She almost forgot the pizza, it was such a stupid thing to do—eating another dinner at almost ten o'clock at night. She made a U-turn and pulled into the parking lot, but she wasn't the only person who'd forgotten. The owner's son was sponging off tables, saying that nobody'd phoned in an order. She wondered if she should just ask for a small plain pizza and get points with her aunt, but she decided no—her aunt could really do without a pizza. She bought a ginger ale in a bottle that exploded all over her when she unscrewed the cap. "Shit!" she said, which brought the owner to the counter. His son shrugged, acknowledging what had happened, but making no comment. "So what's this? Did you shake the bottle?" Mister Rogers said. It wasn't his real name, it was his nickname, behind his back, because he always said "Beautiful day" to adults, and T. G. had pointed out that Mister Rogers said, "It's a beautiful day in the neighborhood." Or, at least, the guy who imitated him on the old *Saturday Night Live* did.

She shook her head. A question like that didn't even deserve a response. The guys did that, sometimes. Would she do it? A girl?

Then came the very loud sound of shattering glass. She ducked, thinking a car was coming in right through the front windows. Mister Rogers and his son ducked, too, and the sponge flew across the room. Mister Rogers quickly got out of his crouch and ran toward the door.

There stood Ms. Nementhal. In a halter top and blue Bermuda shorts, Ms. Nementhal was wincing, her arms clasping her shoulders, her mouth agape. Someone had thrown bottles out of a car window, lots of them, it turned out. Could it have been on purpose? Who littered that way anymore? One had made a huge crack in one of the front windows. "Oh, Jesus," the owner's son moaned. "Are you okay?" he said to Ms. Nementhal.

"What was that?" she said, hysterically. "WHAT WAS THAT?"

"Trash. Every year it's worse trash," Mister Rogers said. "You're all right, ma'am? Is that a little cut on your leg?"

"Shit, shit, shit," the owner's son said, tapping his cell phone. "That was probably that pond scum, Winston Bales." He turned away. Behind Ms. Nementhal were several broken bottles, their necks scattered in one direction, glass strewn across the parking lot. There was a cut on her leg. She was bent over, examining it, her long hair obscuring any expression, and she hadn't responded to the question. She hadn't said one thing, though everybody knew she could monologue for hours. The owner must not know who she was. How would he? Some kid from Yale with her first summer job (as the newspaper report would later inform everyone), a volunteer in a program for troubled teens. They were not troubled! They weren't! Jocelyn had not had the program advertised to her that way. What, exactly, was she troubled about?

One thing would be having to finish her essay, trying to write in a way that was credible about Earth being reversed with the sky; flowers sparkling instead of stars, the stars all fallen around everyone's feet. A *detritus* (was that too big a word?) of stars. What would she be going for, though? Was that just another C-plus idea, or would something like that be Magical Realism?

Well, she knew a grackle when she saw one. Recently, flying squirrels had gotten into the attic and multiplied like crazy, the animal control guy going up every day on the ladder to check the traps until seventeen of them were caught. The mother, then the only remaining baby, old enough to go to college and drink beer if it had been human, were the last to go. They were billed by the day.

Birds! What's happening here? Might a storm be on the way?

Tinkle, tinkle. Then nothing. One more bird flying into the tree, two of the three already lifting off, one landing on the lawn and making the sound over and over, standing there in the grass. No more tinkling sound, no more pseudo-wind-chime susurration, but really: how dumb could she be? It was there, in the blue recycling bin, still filled with wine bottles, seltzer bottles, milk containers, a crushed Budweiser can she'd picked up out of the road (they were not the sort to drink Budweiser) the day before. Also in the recycling bin, where dirty water pooled in a corner, was a tiny fledgling, every now and then beating its wings futilely, voicing an almost silent burble. Right there in the dark water that was probably mostly rainwater, mixed with a bit of undrunk red wine, a splash of Coke that leaked out when the can was tossed. The little bird just looked like an animated piece of crap, its nondescript color that of sludge, some pollen dusting the tops of the bottles and cans, a small fallen branch across one corner like those old-fashioned picture darts her mother used to lick to stick her baby pictures in an album. There had been hundreds of them, but the photographic record fizzled out pretty much where it should have: with her, knobby-kneed, pigtailed, and ribboned, on the steps outside the building where she went to kindergarten.

You weren't supposed to touch birds, because they wouldn't be allowed back in the nest, right? If you got your human smell on them. Or was that an old wives' tale? Were there still old wives who told tales, or did everyone know everything now, including how to remove red wine stains, how to make your tablecloth soft, how to keep salt from getting moist in the container? Oh, it was a world of rice now, very little ingested because quinoa was so popular, that and tabouli and spelt, though rice grains were still put in saltshakers. Rice was still thrown at weddings. Certain weddings.

Poor little dirty sad frightened bird! Poor distraught elders! They all feared the worst scenario: death by drowning; death by starvation; an ugly end with no one but them as witnesses, and they could do nothing except send up a storm of sound and hope either the gods, or the humans who acted like gods, would do the right thing, that one of them would be the savior. She was obviously that, staring nervously for only a few seconds before dropping everything, checking her impulse to plunge in her hand, running inside for the oven mitts, guaranteed to be safe for food cooked up to 450 degrees.

Into the house she ran, out of the house she ran, hands in mitts. But she didn't want to crush it. It was so small. So sodden. The skin of its tiny head looked like the crow's-feet fanning out from the corners of her eyes.

The birds were making a terrible sound, two on the ground as if facing off with her, yet much too far away. Two others sitting high up in the tree were making the loudest noise. She was capable of reaching in, even though the mitts made the use of her hands awkward, to say the least, and lifting out the little thing and putting it on the walkway, where she hoped all traces of Roundup were gone from the spraying done by the lawn service, to keep weeds from sprouting in the sand between bricks . . . maybe put it on the grass. Though it looked like it would need all the traction it could get. What was the scenario? She could retreat to the house or go to the car and turn on the AC and watch in her rearview mirror to see Mother Bird swoop down and—however she did it—enfold Baby Bird somehow, and lift it again to the nest, which she imagined she saw—either that or some dead leaves—midtree. Well, it was nature. It would work out. Of course it would. She kept focusing on the near future because the little bird was cupped in her oven mitts now. When suddenly she remembered something she had forgotten for . . . well, for most of her life. It was a poem that began "Goodbye, little fledgling, fly away." Her grandmother, who'd been such a good baker, had placed in the center of her famous apple pies made with three kinds of apples a little black bird with an open beak, a pie bird, to release steam. A simplified version of a bird, a little objet, the clever baker's secret to a perfect pie.

It was standing there. It was either shivering or trying to move its wet wings. It could have died in the recycling. What if she'd hurried on, thought the happy birds were just voicing their happy songs? Both birds had now flown from the lawn back into the tree. One kept flying up and landing exactly where it had started from. Surely it had a plan? The little bird was slightly lopsided. It made a motion resembling a hop. It opened its beak and made a slightly louder sound than it had made in the blue plastic recycling container, which seemed to alarm it and make it tilt farther sideways. She was overstaying her welcome. Car plan: she scooped up her purse and bag, still wearing the cumbersome silver oven mitts. That was the way she looked as she emerged from under the bower of wisteria, making it a point not to torture herself by looking back, and greeted the man in the open-doored mail truck, only slightly surprised to have come upon her looking the way she did: rather frantic, breathing heavily, her hands like lobster claws immobilized by thick rubber bands.

Regardless of her grandmother's lessons and always gently delivered advice, she'd never made a pie in her life.

AUNT SOPHIE
RENALDO BROWN

Years ago, I saw two people at a summer party who arrived in grand style and departed to everyone's protestations that they shouldn't drive. The driver of the little MG was called Walrus, which I thought was the funniest name I'd ever heard, and his ladyfriend was called Star. She'd been an extra in a few movies but never managed to have a career in Hollywood. Someone at the party said she was a secretary at a recording studio, and someone else said she'd eloped with a much older man and never had the marriage annulled, and that he looked out for her. These people had hardly turned their backs when the gossip began. Someone said to me that it was like everyone lying and conjecturing at Gatsby's parties, but I had not at that point read the book.

Aunt Sophie Renaldo Brown was wearing red sling-back high heels and khaki shorts (hardly Gatsby attire, as I'd later learn) and a tight lavender blouse, under which she wore a push-up bra and, inside the bra, carefully placed, two metal wire champagne cork baskets to suggest hugely protruding nipples. As Sophie Renaldo, she'd been a teetotaler, but after getting her life together, divorcing Roy Renaldo, and eventually a subsequent marriage that lasted six months but gave her the name Brown, matriculating at NYU, she'd developed a taste for icy cold rosé. You know how it is: you get a cat; the cat needs toys; you get a bell so the cat won't kill birds and also a cushion so the cat can rest comfortably somewhere other than on the sofa. A cat becomes a whole big deal. She did have such a cat, named Methuselah by her first ex-husband, who'd believed that the cat was eight or nine years old when they got it from the shelter (this is what they'd been told), and then it had lived another nineteen years and was still going strong except for a recent bout of hypergrooming in the tail area.

Roy was happy to leave the animal behind with Sophie when he moved to York, Maine, to work at an accounting firm with an old Navy friend. He was not so happy to have to continue to pay his soon-to-be-ex-wife's tuition, but the following year she graduated with a degree in sociology. She was currently a hostess at a busy, successful Upper West Side restaurant. She got up early in the morning to walk the cat on a leash (people stared), to buy a small bottle of freshly squeezed orange juice, then return home to sip it as she took her daily vitamins and wrote lengthy passages in her diary. Bryce, the new waiter, often stopped by to round her up for the three-block walk to Café Anywhere. He was the one who'd introduced her to rosé.

My father called her a lush and would have nothing to do with her once she was divorced from his brother—when she became more of an exhibitionist than ever. At her first wedding, she'd constantly raised her wedding gown to show the garter with its thinly braided white ribbons whose little satin pigtail points were dusted with blue sparkles and tiny, dangling heart-shaped crystals. She told me they were edible! She had quite a sense of humor. I was seven years old, and absolutely mesmerized. Who could believe Uncle Roy would find such a prize? His other girlfriends had been heavier, and none had had such luxurious hair, and certainly none had giggled or offered to take me to Central Park. One had asthma.

I was seventeen when Roy and Sophie separated and eighteen when they divorced. They'd never had children, but I always knew she wished I was hers. Sometimes when I was growing up, she'd point to little boys on the street and say she was glad she wasn't stuck with one of them. I usually agreed, because they always seemed wound up and they tended to breathe through their mouths and to have dirt or food on their faces.

I was eighteen when I saw her with the champagne baskets protruding beneath her blouse. She was absolutely straight-faced, because she was good at pulling a joke. She'd taught me not to pop my eyes like my mother and then immediately look down if we saw somebody strange or outlandish. She explained that their appearance might be intentionally funny, and we wouldn't want to appear unsophisticated and react negatively to the joke. Of course the majority of people just passed us by, but I tended to take her word for which of those people intended to be funny with their attire and which didn't.

She could tell instantly whether someone was aware she was dressed ludicrously or was just a loser. Even weird, old-fashioned hats didn't confuse Aunt Sophie. To me, the length of the feather or the amount of swirled netting or the rhinestone clips were indecipherable, but she could tell if a man dressed as a woman in line at the drugstore was kidding or serious. She explained that it would be rude to laugh at a man who thought he looked nice. Little old ladies—the ones that came out of certain apartment buildings—she discounted as being in a time warp. Age was a big factor in whether someone was putting on the audience, but I didn't see clearly, as she did, whether someone was fifty or seventy; they just looked old.

She coached me, but it seemed like almost every case was different and I would never have an eye for nuance. She dressed a lot of different ways herself, though I never saw her wear a hat. Sophie wore high heels, kitten heels, ballet flats in wild colors, tennis shoes, and espadrilles. When she went to work, she favored platform slings, though she sometimes wore red Keds and put on stiletto heels when she got to work. In her opinion, shoes were something people did not kid about. They might buy a dress because they knew it was ridiculously girlie, or wear a color such as bright orange that was meant to shock. But whatever shoes they had on, they weren't joking: ugly shoes they knew to be ugly shoes, though thank heavens it had become as fashionable to wear ugly shoes as attractive ones—or really any kind of shoe you wanted. Many kinds of shoes cut across class lines, such as clogs with closed backs. Nurses wore them, waitresses wore them, but so did college students and rich ladies walking their little dogs on the Upper West Side (East Side shoes were totally different). I pretty much understood Sophie's point, but I still found certain distinctions hard to make. Boots? She explained that because they always cost so much, boots automatically conveyed wealth. Sophie granted my point that if we were somewhere else, there might be some confusion about boots, but the bottom line was that they were not working-class footwear in New York City. Also, you had to invest a lot of time in breaking them in, so however strange they looked—reptilian or gold-cap-toed, bright purple with stacked heels—they were never a joke joke.

I kept it in the back of my mind that if I married Bryce Seward (I had such a crush on him), I'd just ask Sophie to pick out absolutely everything I'd wear on my wedding day. I had previously thought I might marry McGann O'Marra and Jerry Underwood—in fifth and sixth grade, respectively. Then came the long stretch of believing that I would never marry anyone. That no one would ever want to marry me. All Jerry Underwood really wanted to do, it was clear to me, was to draw concentric circles around my budding breasts with Magic Marker. It took forever to fade, and I had to make sure my mother never saw me naked. My father would have killed him, and that's not an exaggeration. Anyway—this gets me back to where I began, more or less: Aunt Sophie and the little wire champagne baskets.

She did this at the garden party, which was held at a big house in Maine nearly five hours from New York, on a river. She told us she'd called ahead to make absolutely sure that Roy, her first ex-husband, wouldn't be there, but I thought that, secretly, she would have liked running into him. The couple giving the party had told her that she was "fun" and that they hadn't kept up with Roy, let alone invited him to the party. She remembered these people only slightly, from a dinner she'd had with them at a restaurant when they'd all been offered a room at the hotel across the street if they'd leave. She loved to tell people how scandalously she and her friends acted, though you could never press her and get details.

Inside, I saw something I thought was a piece of sculpture. Closer inspection revealed it to be a great quantity of cooked lobsters stacked on the shelves of a tall metal stand surrounded not by devotional candles but by open jars of mayonnaise. At that point, I don't think I even knew lobsters existed; I was fascinated by their bright red shells. Wasn't this more of an adventure than going on another pointless coffee date with Les Allan? Sure—everything I did with Aunt Sophie was exciting and new, though getting up at six in the morning in order to set out before seven had made me feel a little faint. I rode in the back of the car with Bryce's boyfriend, Nathaniel, and the cat, who was stretched out in a cage with one of Sophie's old bed pillows for a cushion and a cone around its head so it couldn't overgroom its tail. Aunt Sophie rode in the passenger seat, map in hand, her eyes shadowed in silvery green powder, the lashes thick with mascara, even though you could see dark raccoon circles under her eyes. She turned around often to talk to us. I was so excited to be going to a garden party—whatever that was. For one thing, they were rich people who had a big lawn—this much I figured out from what Sophie said about them. The Boyfriend kept saying that so much driving wasn't his idea of a good Sunday, and Bryce and Sophie both said, almost in unison, that the words *good* and *Sunday* were an oxymoron. Sundays were boring; they signified the last-minute desperation of having a good weekend. The two of them were united in their scorn of Sunday. To them, the day meant nothing but news-print on their fingertips and eggs prepared with glutinous, highly caloric sauces. Sundays were always straining after fun, like a horse being whipped to win the race, when fun came naturally during the rest of the week. Sundays carried a burden too heavy to bear.

Bryce was wearing a white shirt and tight jeans with a few little slashes on the thighs (and this was way before anyone did such a thing). He wore sandals a friend had brought him from Morocco. The Boyfriend had on madras Bermuda shorts and a navy blue Lacoste shirt and leather sneakers with tan colored laces and tan socks folded over at the ankle. He had very hairy legs. He worked at another restaurant—more like a bar—in Chelsea. He'd graduated from Juilliard but had some sort of breakdown and couldn't play music or lis-ten to any female vocalists. No one dared to turn on the car radio. Methuselah kept trying to stand in the cage, although all the turns in the road kept knocking him down, making his bell ring, and sometimes provoking long, weak cries of protest. I was wearing a wrap dress in a nice shade of gray that I'd bought at a flea market on Amsterdam Avenue for next to nothing and black patent-leather ankle-strap inch-high heels. It seemed pretty radical not to wear any jewelry, so I didn't. The rumor was that Leo Lerman (who apparently wrote about the arts) was going to be at the party, and also a famous painter. I didn't catch his name, but the Boyfriend clearly thought he was an idiot and that the party wasn't worth going to, even if it was Sunday and there was nothing better to do. He refused in advance to do any of the driving, and he insisted that we stop every two hours so he could pee. He was the first person I heard worrying aloud about bedbugs. He wouldn't go to the movies because he was afraid bedbugs might be in the theater seats.

Now I have to tell the rest of the story another way, because I can't keep pretending that what happened didn't happen. It was this: we found a parking spot under a willow tree and left the windows down so Methuselah would be okay. Walking to the party, with my arm linked through Aunt Sophie's, and the Boyfriend and the man who I now understood would never, ever be my husband, Sophie said, "I went to have my yearly mammogram, and they saw something. I have to go into the hospital on Tuesday afternoon and have it biopsied. If anything happens to me, I want you to promise to take care of Methuselah. I know I should say everything's going to be okay, but I've got a premonition that it isn't. Do you promise?"

This was bad news, said so matter-of-factly that, right away, I began silently denying it. Did Bryce know about this? Whether the Boyfriend was aware of it didn't matter even slightly. Did my mother know? That was important. If she did, then maybe she could reassure me, because it was clear Sophie wasn't going to. On the other hand, if she didn't know, would I have to tell her? Or, worse yet, keep quiet about it? Sophie said, "Bryce is going to walk Methuselah for me after my biopsy." (So he did know!) "I'll have to miss that day at work, but maybe I can go in the next day. Look at that man over there, peeing against a tree. He thinks we don't see him. The party must already be in full swing!"

I looked in the same direction but didn't see anyone. "Right there!" she said, pointing. There were many trees. I squinted a little, though I didn't really want to see a man peeing. But then I did see him: a guy tucking his penis inside his pants, turning and walking quickly away. "That didn't even happen at the party at the Great Gatsby's," she said. "But I guess you can't expect him to put everything in one book. I'll write about it in my diary: that it was an omen. Fate was pissing on me."

At least, I think that's what she said. Methuselah was crying. We both turned and looked at the car, but now it was quiet.

"I think I'll have a smoke. You go in and I'll join you in a minute," the Boyfriend said.

"I'll stay with you," Bryce said. "We'll see you girls soon."

We walked ahead, still arm in arm. I hadn't answered her about the cat. I hadn't said anything sympathetic or helpful or even acknowledged that I'd heard what she'd told me. I couldn't think what to say. I, too, trusted her instincts. I couldn't imagine life without her. And to be honest, I'd always had to fake it about liking Methuselah. I didn't want to be a young old maid who lived alone with her cat. The thought of it resulted in tears filling my eyes. I wiped them quickly away with my free hand as Star exited the party barefoot, with lobsters raised like free weights above her head, and was chased, giggling, around the side of the house. I never saw either of them again, though I once saw a man with a similar mustache I mistook for Walrus when I was checking out of a CVS a couple of years later.

Another car bumped onto the grassy area: a Mustang convertible with a Vermont license plate, music playing loudly, an old Sinéad O'Connor song, "Nothing Compares 2 U." The driver and a woman in the passenger seat were laughing loudly, enjoying every tree root the car bumped over, the woman holding her sequined baseball cap to her head in an exaggerated way. So was her hat a joke? Why were so many women at the party wearing hats? Was Aunt Sophie serious in what she was suddenly saying about Bryce and Nathaniel intending to hook up with the man who'd been peeing against a tree? I turned to see Nathaniel cupping his hand around a match to light a cigarette, and Bryce stretching, slowly lowering his hands down his thighs to his knees, then lower, bending further. Was it a kind of preening, or just a postdrive stretch? A puff of smoke went up in the air. I wanted to be that smoke. To disappear. Instead, I listened from afar to my own voice as I lied about my affection for the cat. I let go of her arm. She brushed her hand lightly down my long hair I was too stupid to know was attractive to men, though later I practiced tossing it in front of a mirror. Aunt Sophie's heels were higher than anyone else's I'd seen—certainly higher than mine—but she walked briskly, with confidence. How did a person have confidence if they didn't believe in the future? I wondered. In an hour or so, Aunt Sophie would be placing the little metal baskets inside her blouse, seeming to be having a good time, shocking people but making them laugh.

It was a rocky road to death, full of bumps and obstacles, with low-hanging branches that would slap you in the face if you didn't duck, and there was always the danger that the underside of the car might sink deeply into a pothole and bottom out, leaving us all stranded. You could call for help, but how to describe where we were, surrounded by trees that blocked out the sun, an anonymous place at the end of an unpaved road, where man pissed on nature and puffed carcinogens into the air, sending up smoke signals to mix with the clouds.

The Boyfriend knew how to blow smoke rings. It was amazing for a few seconds until he stopped pursing his lips, silently puffing out the message of the day, and of every day: O, O, O.

ADIRONDACK CHAIRS

After Artigan's death, Bea was afraid to weed the garden. Artigan had not died from the yellow jacket bites—though he was horribly allergic—but because as his shovel split their in-ground nest and they swarmed up as the first and last golden tornado he'd ever see, he fell backward over the stone wall and hit his head on a tree stump. Artigan had been doing some gardening for summer people who were not yet occupying their house. The blood was congealing when Bea arrived in the Heppendales' truck to pick him up. She worked at the greenhouse, where there'd been a big run on lemon verbena. She and Tracy (who'd once worked at a vineyard in Sonoma) had come up with the idea that the greenhouse could offer a free wine tasting with music and gardening information. There was a tip jar, and they were a little embarrassed that people left so much.

I worked at the greenhouse, too, but I never had any bright ideas. The Heppendales raised my friends' hourly wage and agreed that, yes, they should offer the back building for weddings. Alex Heppendale ordered Bea and Tracy new gardening boots from Zappos, along with a one-hundred-dollar gift certificate each for another pair of shoes. By July, when word had spread about the cocktails and gardening advice, business had almost doubled. Chilean chardonnay, supercold, in real glasses, with hors d'oeuvres and Mr. Heppendale and his daughter Alex (a Princeton graduate) circulating and offering tips about gardening . . . people in town went mad for it, as well as people from away. Mrs. Heppendale bought flouncy dresses and meant to attend, but found that, Friday after Friday, she had a headache.

On Saturdays, Artigan also worked at the greenhouse, tending the suddenly popular, slightly strange herbs and re-potting orchids. Had he not died, he and Bea were going to test out the back building for their own wedding at the end of August. They'd already been a couple long enough for him to teach her to drive, for her to break his texting addiction, for them to consider sponsoring a child from the Fresh Air Fund the following summer, by which time they'd be legit. As a little girl Bea had believed in angels, but that was more or less because she loved girlie tchotchkes. My Little Pony was over the top, but even as she got older, she kept her fondness for barrettes decorated with sunflowers and bunches of cherries. Her hair was seventeen inches long, measured from the crown to its longest point. (Tracy had the idea, and I measured. I admit, we thought a lot about ourselves and very little about plants on our half-hour lunch breaks.)

At the ER, there was much commotion, little talk. People either pulled Bea forward by her hand like a child or repeatedly dropped her hand, she couldn't remember. She knew when she saw him on the grass near the garden that he was dead. She'd seen enough corpses on TV. She had no religious beliefs, so she didn't think Artigan was anywhere but there, and as she dialed 911, she knew he'd only be on the ground a few minutes longer. So much for their wedding.

I quit my other job waiting tables at the York Harbor Inn and stepped in full-time to join Tracy at the greenhouse at the end of July, when it became clear Bea wasn't going to be able to work anymore. It wasn't just grief, it was morning sickness. She wouldn't have to borrow a child from Fresh Air to play with on the beach the following summer. Of course she wasn't going to be able to afford to live in town anymore. She'd only been able to do it because a former college room-mate had offered Artigan his cousin's house for the summer while the estate was being settled. In exchange for gardening and lawn mowing, Artigan and Bea had briefly seemed like everybody else, sitting on the front lawn in the Adirondack chairs, admiring the bobbly headed peonies that dowsed the ground, drinking a G and T in the evening (which, for them, meant eight o'clock). When Bea's mother and father came to take her home, they stripped the beds and wrote thank-you notes to the family (strangely, using no salutation). They also turned the Adirondack chairs upside down on the front lawn as if they were boats that needed to drain. My aunt and uncle, who had a lot more money than my parents, once had a maid who was intent on showing you that she'd cleaned the rugs, so she put them back upside down. Sometimes the colors were surprisingly bright. Once or twice they were left wrong side up.

At the Heppendales' greenhouse, Tracy and I were really the also-rans. I was always tripping over the hose or putting a plant down too hard and cracking the clay pot. She fainted, on a hot August day, loading a ten-pound bag of soil into some old guy's trunk. After that she made sure to hydrate and wore the big canvas sun hat with the annoying chin strap. She told me later it was weird to have felt the way Artigan might have just before he died. We'd both gone to the funeral, though Bea wasn't there. It was my second and Tracy's first. It was a hot day and Mrs. Heppendale hadn't been there because she'd had an allergic reaction to something she ate the night before. For one reason or another, Mrs. Heppendale was hardly ever anywhere.

It was the turned-over chairs at Artigan and Bea's that really stopped Tracy and me when we went over to the house to see if Bea and her parents needed any help. When we got there, though, they'd already left. We pulled up the steep driveway and went in through the back, so we didn't see the chairs at first, though we did see and read the notes from Bea's mother and father, with a box of Kleenex weighing down the corner of one and a conch shell as a paperweight over the other, both smack in the middle of the dining room table, bracketed by silver candlesticks. What was going to happen to Bea? She was almost certainly going to be okay, we figured, but that was before we knew about the pregnancy and before scuzzy Winston Bales blabbed that she'd been known to do a little coke. The Zappos boots, in a striped pattern with the stripes filled in with paisley, sat by the back door. Another empty box had been discarded in the trash: stilettos, said the print on the box, black patent, size 7½. She must have taken them. To do what? Stumble around in her pregnancy? Bea's family lived in Jersey City, New Jersey. Her mother worked for a dry cleaner. Her father was an accountant. One of his clients had been Big Pussy, from *The Sopranos*. Shortly after Bea's departure, Mrs. Heppendale also left. She told people she was going to visit her sister in London, but both Alex and Mr. Heppendale said that it was a made-up story, that she was simply walking out on them. Part of her reason was that they were obsessed with Bea, and inconsolably distraught about Artigan, while they'd paid no attention to her when she had the flu, or when her migraines began (she'd had to get a cab to the ER). Also, her husband and daughter danced outside on the terrace under the stars to big-band music piped out through those excellent Bose speakers they had everywhere, and she was worried that anyone seeing such a thing would think something incestuous was going on.

I was the last one to see Mrs. Heppendale. I was at the transportation center in Portsmouth, waiting for my best friend since first grade to arrive by bus from Logan airport. She'd just been given a Tiffany engagement ring. She was coming for a visit to show it off and to take me to dinner with her fiancé's American Express card, to which she'd been added. Things were going to work out for Stella. Hers wasn't going to be any tragic situation. I'd gotten my hair highlighted and was wearing new ballet flats. Stella had the same shoes—everybody that summer had those shoes—but hers were bright yellow.

Suddenly out of nowhere came Mrs. Heppendale, as the bus was visible in the distance. Well, she came from inside, but she just appeared, big zippered bag slung over one shoulder (she traveled light), purse in hand. "How interesting that, as I exit, I encounter the budding writer," she said to me. "I'm going to England and not coming back. I've got a sister there who loves me, and I love the theater. It hasn't been easy, seeing summer productions in barns full of mosquitoes and minor TV actresses at the Ogunquit Playhouse in revivals of *The Sound of Music*. There's not much of a story in my running away, because once you say I drink, no one's going to be interested or sympathetic. I thought you were a nice girl, though seriously lacking in self-confidence. I never understood why you hung on Bea's every word. You and everybody else thought she was so great. I thought she was scared of her own shadow and that she tried to cover that by being outgoing. Did she and Arty ever really seem to be in love? I never thought so. But I'm quite a bit older than you girls, so I'm not preoccupied with love. All I care about anymore is mysteries and crossword puzzles. And by the way, I know more about orchids than any of them. I kept telling them to stop repotting. Orchids are best grown in the smallest possible pot, you know. All they care is that they're fashionable and that they'll sell well. That's why we stocked those ceramic kissing frog couples and hoses made to look like cobra skin." She gave a little snort.

How had she gotten to the transportation center? Had she driven and left her car in the parking lot, or had someone dropped her off? She said, "There's a species of orchid in Australia—only in Australia—a subterranean species that blooms underground. It has no chlorophyll, but it flowers beneath the soil. It's a perfect metaphor for something, isn't it? Use it sometime, and think of me."

"Mrs. Heppendale. You're really leaving? Right now?"

"If the bus ever arrives," she said.

The bus was swinging around the curve to pull into its bay. An announcement of its arrival came over the PA system.

"I'm sorry we never really got to know each other," I said. "You know, Bea and I liked working at the greenhouse. I think you would have liked Bea if, you know, you'd known her. Better, I mean."

"I don't like people who flirt. I know people enjoy flirting and being flirted with. It's just not my thing."

"Bea flirted?" I said.

"With Alex! She was quite intent on getting something going with Alex. I was the one who had to point it out to my own daughter. What do you girls notice? Pain concentrates the mind, I suppose. When I have migraines I have to remember to breathe and to focus through them. You squint whether you want to or not. Nobody could be more surprised than me that sometimes I can see right to the heart of things. That's no doubt what made me think to tell you about that orchid."

"Did Alex, I mean, she agreed with you?"

Mrs. Heppendale raised an eyebrow. "She's not a total fool when something is made clear," she said.

"What do you see when you look at me?" I said.

What I saw, with my inner eye, was a young woman too often stunned, even by the most usual things: two chairs left behind at a borrowed house, in an odd position. A note in backward-sloping handwriting, another note more or less block-printed, all in capital letters, lying on a table where a fruit bowl might be.

39

Mrs. Heppendale said nothing, though she must have said good-bye, because our eyes locked for a few seconds before she stepped onto the bus. Then suddenly Stella, the Luckiest Girl in the World (self-appointed), exited through the rear door and flew into my arms. What if Mrs. Heppendale saw that? Stella's hair smelled of peaches. The diamond ring sparkled as if the day weren't cloudy. I looked over Stella's shoulder. I couldn't see through the bus windows, though I'd ridden that bus and knew Mrs. Heppendale could see out. Was she wondering what my next expression would be, how soon I'd drop my polite but nervous smile?

Bea had had a flirtation with Alex? It had gone right by me. What would something like that mean, anyway? Nothing. It's not like they ended up together. (By September, even Stella's engagement was broken; instead of returning the ring, she'd sold it to an estate jeweler in Boston and sent the money to him—which, of course, was nowhere near as much as he'd paid for the ring.)

In a supermarket recently, I stopped to look at the orchids and thought about telling the guy who worked in the floral section about the underground orchid, though I realized he'd probably think I was either crazy or flirting. I wasn't the sort of person who struck up conversations with strangers. Bea had been the one who was outgoing, always curious, asking whether I believed in God; what I expected out of life; how high I thought a heel could be before it just looked silly. "You take it on faith that there's a God?" she'd echoed one time, wide-eyed. Well, sure. The same way we take it on faith that people in the Adirondacks must sit in those uncomfortable wooden chairs with the seats tilted so deeply backward that your knees sprang up like a ventriloquist's dummy as the wood pressed into the back of your thighs. Otherwise, why would they be so named?

I thought about Bea a lot, but she never answered my e-mails, and her cell phone had been disconnected. One time when my thoughts were wandering, it suddenly came to me what Bea's parents had done. When they left the house, they'd turned the Adirondack chairs over (shocking pink was that summer's color) to show that they disliked them. They'd given the finger to the very symbol of summer, and they'd been right to do it. Those things ruined women's stockings and made you spill your drink; you had to sit in them awk-wardly, pretending that your casual moment was also com-fortable. That you'd adapted easily to their too-deep seats and were having fun.

I certainly wouldn't know how to write the story of that summer. Tracy and Bea and Alex and I were at those points in our lives when everything made sense in not making sense, you know? You do know. Who hasn't been twenty-one? Who hasn't sat outdoors on a summer night and known—known without questioning it—that through the impenetrable black sky, someone or something is looking down at you? The stars just glitter to draw your attention.

because I've tripped or fallen a couple of times, and once had to wear a soft cast. And because I spend so much time and money having her cared for. They're distressed that if I can't get a tick off her on the first pull, I drive her to the vet. I've explained that the vet does not charge me for this, but that seems to be the least of the problem. It's that I'm in the car too often and that my life is "centered around the dog." God help me if they ever find out Yancey and I sometimes split a microwaved chicken burrito for dinner. I wash it down with a glass of white wine, Yancey with a small bowl of milk.

Don't worry: I do have a topic of conversation other than the dog.

I'm going to tell you something funny—if anyone thinks anything about the IRS might be even remotely funny. It's that they sent someone to the house to look at the room I use for writing poetry. They did not believe, from the photographs my accountant sent, that the door was really on hinges, and that the room had no other use. We weren't lying. The room—which used to be the little sewing room of the lady we bought the house from, which I used for storage before I decided I didn't need anything that was stored there and gave it all away—contains my desk, with a typewriter and the usual things that one has on one's desk, such as a bowl of paper clips and a jar of pens. There's a kilim with excessive knotted fringe that's faded horribly in the sunlight. There are bookshelves filled with poetry books, essays, criticism, et cetera. The broken fax machine sits on a little stool that also holds the orchid from what used to be the big greenhouse in town, until the owner's wife left him and he moved away to Tampa. Ginger maintains that I overwater it. The low light and the cold will kill it. And it isn't helped by Yancey pouncing on it, mistaking it, with her blurred vision, for her favorite toy, which is a squeaking Ed Grimley doll.

The man from the IRS was nice. He helped me push up a storm window and lower the screen, and he stood by while I vacuumed up dead flies. From his posture, I suspected he'd been to military school, or at least in the service, and I turned out to be right. He'd gone to VMI, he told me. We talked a little about Lexington, a southern town we both liked. He was probably used to people trying to get on his good side, but when you have anything as real as a small southern town between you, a few words of reminiscence aren't likely to be mistaken for buttering up.

He admired the framed Audubon prints on the wall going up the stairs. I pointed to the black half circle below them, which he'd been kind enough not to mention. It got there because my husband, who drank, took a fall one night and went over backward, the rubber sole of his shoe scraping a near-perfect arc underneath the prints. The fall didn't kill him, though driving into a tree did. Anyway, I told my visitor about the mark on the wall before we got to the landing. I had him precede me because I don't bound up the stairs anymore. "But you do use your room regularly," he said. I thought he was perhaps speaking sympathetically, cuing me. I used it every day, so agreeing was only telling the truth.

He saw that the door was on the hinges. That even the small closet held typing paper and a file drawer filled with rough drafts, not clothes. He admired the rug, which pleased me. He seemed like a genuine person, if you know what I mean. Yancey clicked along beside us, with her long toenails that the vet kept urging me to let her cut, though I know Yancey hates it so much, I've demurred. The IRS man said that his wife had a poodle that had been run over by a truck. Whether it was a standard poodle or one of those little things, he didn't say. I told him I was sorry and waited for a signal we might leave the room. He took a few steps forward and looked out the window. Below, the white lilacs were blooming. He said, "When Lilacs Last in the Dooryard Bloom'd!" It crossed my mind that he might be testing. Of course I knew who wrote the poem. I wasn't, for example, pretending that my husband's office was mine, to continue to take the deduction after his death. So I said the poet's name. Then we stood there a bit longer.

"You know, this is a peaceful, functional room," he said. "More people should have a sanctuary like this. It must bring you pleasure to walk into this room."

I'd been warned by the accountant to volunteer as little as possible, so I just said, "Yes, it does."

"Not even a desk phone. A room for uninterrupted time."

I nodded. That was entirely right. There was a phone in the kitchen and an extension phone in the bedroom that Étienne called an "antique." She'd told me more than once that if I wanted to get a new phone, she could get good money for my pale blue Princess phone on eBay. I'm not rich, but I don't have to sell every small thing I have. I give most of it away, or put a few things in my nice young neighbor's July tag sale. That was not the issue, though. My extension phone was perfectly fine.

"I see that it's your office," he said matter-of-factly. "It's certainly just as you said it was. I hope you're getting good writing done in here. I know you've had quite a few poems published in recent years. My daughter is at Sarah Lawrence, and she's explained to me that poetry writing doesn't bring in much income. Totally separate from knowing about my seeing you today, I mean. She wants to be a playwright."

"I think that would be very interesting," I said sincerely. I tried not to miss any production that wasn't a musical at Hackmatack Playhouse, in North Berwick. Musicals I can do without. In the evening, I often listen to classical music in the living room. Yancey is soothed by it. Really, nothing is so lovely as a quietly snoring dog and some evening Brahms, as you sit in a comfortably overstuffed chair with your feet on the footstool.

"My house looks like a tornado hit it!" he said. "Your husband drank? My wife drinks. Our daughter could have had a very good scholarship at a nearby college, but she insisted on going away, and I knew exactly why. Last year when I had my appendix out, my wife forgot to pick me up when I was discharged. I had to get a cab home. And do you know what she was doing, that she'd lost track of time? She was having a gin and tonic in the middle of the afternoon, painting our daughter's bedroom bright yellow, to make it 'cheerful.' She just painted whatever area of the wall was available to her. She didn't move any furniture. She painted around the headboard. It was quite a mess. It made me feel faint when I saw it."

I knew this conversation would not be taking place if I'd allowed the accountant to come to the house the same day the man from IRS came, but I hate it when people stand there like I'm a young, helpless girl again, and that inevitably happens if two people are present, because one of them is bound to feel sorry for you. I'm seventy-seven years old. I've

"Do you prefer reading older poetry, or are you interested in new poetry?"

"Let's say newer. Because I've never read recent poetry at all. We subscribe to magazines that print poetry, but I skip over it. I'm an equal opportunity idiot, I guess you'd say. I don't read cartoon captions either."

"Tell me a little about yourself," I said. "Sentimental? At all mystical? Do you like a poem that tells a story, or a poem that's more of an enigma?"

"I liked Robert Frost when I was at VMI," he said. "I think he would have been the most recent poet we read."

"And I'll bet they taught you all wrong. I'll bet they told you 'The Road Not Taken' was about making important choices and exhibiting free will, didn't they?"

"I don't really remember. I just remember that my roommate got two days in detention because he didn't memorize it."

"Are you Facebook friends now?"

"With Hank? No, he's not on Facebook. He's in jail in Delaware. For menacing his ex-wife."

"My daughter's wife was stalked by her ex-boyfriend. She says there's no connection between her coming out and his doing that, but you have to wonder. He was an awful man. He slit her tires once. There's still a restraining order against him, though they've heard he went back to Chicago."

He shook his head slowly, lips pursed.

"I'll tell you what," I said. "He's not at all like Robert Frost, but I think you might like the poems of James Wright. My favorite poem by him is 'Lying in a Hammock at William Duffy's Farm in Pine Island, Minnesota.'" I held on to the banister and sat on the step. Yancey settled on her haunches next to me. When was this man ever going to leave, when was the door going to open with a great heave, when would the vole have to race into its hole, the snake take a break, the rabbit hide by habit, eyes bright and ears perked to the crackle of grass?

I cleared my throat. Reciting poetry while sitting was a little like trying to sing when flat on your back in bed, but I wanted him to hear the poem, and I'd been standing long enough:

Lying in a Hammock at William Duffy's Farm in Pine Island, Minnesota

Over my head, I see the bronze butterfly,
Asleep on the black trunk,
Blowing like a leaf in green shadow.
Down the ravine behind the empty house,
The cowbells follow one another
Into the distances of the afternoon.
To my right,
In a field of sunlight between two pines,
The droppings of last year's horses
Blaze up into golden stones.
I lean back, as the evening darkens and comes on.
A chicken hawk floats over, looking for home.
I have wasted my life.

"Is that really a poem?" he finally said.

"What else would it be?"

"I've never heard anything like that. The last line comes out of nowhere."

"I don't think so. He could have said that from the beginning, but he gave us the scene so that we'd be seduced, the way he'd been, and then he changed the game on us—on himself—at the last moment."

"That's the kind of guy who'd stick a pin in a balloon!" he said. "I mean, thank you very much for reciting that. I'll get a book of his poetry and write to let you know my reaction."

"That's good," I said. "Any day's good when you get someone to buy a book of poetry who wouldn't ordinarily do it."

"You thought I'd identify with the guy in the hammock," he said. "And I guess I do, to be honest."

"Most people who are being honest feel that way at least some of the time, in my experience."

"I appreciate your asking me to move in," he said.

I smiled. When he left, when the car had safely backed out of the driveway, I'd clip the leash on Yancey and walk her back to the field, then unclip it and let her loose to sniff out the day's still dazzling possibilities. She looked a little kinky in her black booties. And her lovely coat could use a brushing, I saw. No day failed to contain the unexpected. Which I suspect Yancey thought, too, especially because she didn't quite understand why she couldn't make a wild dash like a thunderbolt from door to field, why she panted, why she failed to catch anything, why she'd been skunked, in fact.

Startled starlings flew up out of the high grass, their black whorl a little tornado that did not touch down and therefore did no damage. They disappeared like a momentary perception above Yancey's head, fanning out and flying west. Or like the clotted words crammed into a cartoon bubble. Like one of Ginger's finger-paintings from so, so long ago, brought home for inspection and praise.

SILENT PRAYER

"Sometimes," he said, "I think people would sympathize with me if the roles were reversed and I was a woman whose job required her to travel. Have you thought about it that way? In this time when women have still not gotten the opportunities and respect they should, whereas men—I stand here as a case in point—are criticized for doing what women aspire to do. You'd like me to stay home and help you plan a birthday party for Joshua, which I can do by phone, by sending you e-mail, by doing anything that might represent my share of the work, but you won't give me a break. It's as though I want to go on every business trip. As though the last flight wasn't a nightmare. I had a headache for two days afterwards. Do you have any idea at all where my black Nikes are? Not the Pumas that are mostly black, but the Nikes?"

"I'm sure if we still had your assistant, she could find them."

"What's that supposed to mean? She miscarried and she's

suffering a major depression. She's called off her marriage. She should be here, to locate my shoes? Are you suggesting I'm a monster? What if my wife might know where my favorite shoes are? Even if it's a trivial thing to know."

"LuAnne called and said she'd kept down both dinner last night and lunch. She can't wait to get back here. If you ask me, which nobody ever does, that soccer player wasn't worthy of her and this is all for the best."

"I wonder how other couples talk to each other," he said. "I really do wonder that. But there's no way to find out. You can't believe what you see in the movies or on TV or in books, least of all the so-called reality shows. Maybe Roz Chast has some idea. That's about the only person I can think of."

"I saw a shoe on the back stairs. I have no idea where the other one is. Women don't misplace their shoes."

"Back stairs. Just a minute."

She sat on the bed—king-size, at his insistence; separate reading lights, two night tables with identical spherical digital clocks whose alarms chirped a birdcall. She had to set hers at the highest volume; years ago, when she first came to Maine, she'd trained herself to sleep through the sounds of birds and crickets. Now the sputtering, muffler-missing motorcycles that constantly passed by posed a different sort of challenge: how to resist stringing razor wire across the road.

"Thank you. They were on the back stairs. One shoe was on top of the other."

"Women don't stack their shoes," she said. "You have a way of turning discussions to the differences between men and women. I don't really think about that all the time, but I find I always have to talk about it. Going back to your earlier point, Hughes would do anything possible to keep you, and if you said you were sick of so much flying . . ."

"Hughes and the Genius aren't on the case the way I am, I agree. Why don't you call Hughes and say just that? I wouldn't stop you. I would, however, be angry if it backfired, and he sent me to California more often."

"You can have dinner at Perbacco," she said. "That almost makes it worth it."

He looked at his phone. "Text from LuAnne," he said. "She's going to bed."

"It's not even four o'clock."

"What would you have me do? Text her and tell her to walk around the block and slap her cheeks a few times?"

"Yeah. And communicate all of that with the smiley symbol and lots of exclamation points," she said. "I never wanted a king-size bed. The maid hates putting on the sheets. She spends half of her four hours here being exasperated with the bed. Even when she gets the contour sheet on, she keeps staring at it like it's a field of smoldering embers.

"Remember the time you forgot your driver's license and you missed the flight?" she said. "For about a year I was convinced you'd done it on purpose, to come home when I least expected it, to see what I was doing."

"Excuse me? Wouldn't that have required excessive effort, and might that not indicate some paranoia on your part?"

"Remember what I was doing?"

"I was really upset. I thought I'd lost both my AmEx and my driver's license, and I knew I could grab my passport, but I guess, well, I guess I was feeling paranoid, like someone might have slipped the two most important cards out of—"

"Are you stalling for time because you don't remember what I was doing?"

"Jesus! I remember what you were doing. You'd put some grease all over your hair and were sitting stark naked on the front porch wearing nothing but a shower cap, except that you'd dragged out some huge scarf to cover yourself with if anybody walked by, though I don't know how you could be so sure you'd see them, and you were having a cigarette, the last year you smoked cigarettes."

"I was looking at *Vogue* and drinking a virgin margarita."

"Why do you bring this up?"

"Because what I do is so innocuous. I spend my time thinking about a party at Water Country. I can't even plan our son's birthday by myself. I don't know how to be in the world. How can you stand me?"

"I chose you out of all the world."

"And you keep me by shining that sincere smile on me and constantly implying that men and women are just different, and by managing to convince everybody you're such a good guy because you made your ex-girlfriend from years ago your assistant, even after she had an affair behind your back with Hughes the second she met him, and furthermore I agree with you. She's a very capable, nice person."

"A one-night stand is not an 'ex-girlfriend.' And if we might possibly discuss something else, even though LuAnne is your favorite subject. There's a book, a novel, by that writer who wrote that story you love about Bruns. I heard about it on NPR. In the novel, the character's wife is crazed with the desire to have a child and hops a plane when she knows she'll be fertile and goes to where he and a bunch of friends are gathering because an old friend unexpectedly died—"

"I still can't believe that we had that crazy time together and went off to that house you'd rented in Marin because you probably thought you'd take some other girl there—and we found that croquet set in the garage and set it up and played a game naked when it got dark."

"I'm quite aware of our history. We've now been married for nine, going on ten years. We have a wonderful son. I'm not going to apologize for the next ten years, because apologizing for the first ten has been enough, don't you think? I was having a panic attack. All I said to you in Marin, which I still don't think was so crazy, was that we should back off and think about the relationship for a while."

"What would you have done if Hughes hadn't suddenly appeared on the scene and tempted you to work for his company?"

"I wasn't looking for a job when Hughes got in touch. Were you under the impression that I was? I was actually trying to cut down my hours and build more time into my schedule for tennis."

"What a prig you sound like! Your tennis time! Anybody would think you were vile."

"Vile?"

"I can't believe what I hear sometimes. Like this is a movie of some stupid rich people's lives. We're really sorry the lobstermen can't afford to live in town anymore, and it's really too bad about all the businesses going under—or maybe the greenhouse stays open because they sell orchids, which have become the new azaleas around here—and sure, the economy is fucked. But we know all about French wines and fly first class and think about fucking tennis."

"You, yourself, have thoughts on tennis?"

"That it would be better for me than yoga and Pilates and power walks with weights strapped on my ankles. Jesus! We've got to watch out."

"Okay, you pick up those binoculars and watch out while I'm gone, and if any fashionable sports activities come this way, you hold up a hand and you say, 'None of that here; I'm not having any kicking, or tackling, or kneeing the other guy in the balls.' You keep the house safe, use the gun in the drawer if you have to, to keep us safe from sports, which have become terminally fashionable in your mind, I now understand."

"What gun in what drawer?"

"I was kidding. The water pistol Hughes gave Joshua that you confiscated and keep in the kitchen drawer with the steak knives, for some reason. By the way, I was looking for an unmatched sock and opened your night table drawer and saw you had quite a bit of new La Perla. Expensive stuff!"

"You love to pretend I'm always spending money."

"Really, sometimes you say the most ridiculous things. An aversion to tennis! It's too crazy."

"I don't have an aspersion." She blinked. Why had she said that? The same way she matter-of-factly corrected Joshua, she now corrected herself. "An aversion," she said.

"Then call the coach tomorrow and set up a time."

"You know I'm not going to do that."

"You could."

"You'd hate it if I was all over your territory. It's one of the reasons why you left her, isn't it? Because there wasn't anything you didn't do together and agree on?"

"That question can't be answered. The way you've put it, I mean."

"I don't care if I'm childish," she said. "I'm trapped in this horrible place with my wicked thoughts and a kid who always mixes up words and uses the wrong one, and no money of my own, and a job that's just something to pass the time, and only you have the key to the wine cellar."

A motorcycle passed by, the sound shaking the house. Then came another.

"Wine cellar?" he scoffed.

"Metaphorically speaking."

"Okay," he said. "This is you-know-what, that g word you never want me to say, and I'm not going to say it, I'm just going to give you a hug and hope you snap out of this mood very soon, even if it means you're starkers on the porch, sipping your nonalcoholic drink that you pride yourself so much for drinking, as if I ever thought you were an alcoholic. So come here and we'll embrace and even though I'm not saying you-know-what, you know that I'll be back in three days, and that I love you."

She ran into his arms. His travel bag was suspended from a padded strap over his shoulder; it swayed before steadying itself. If he had facial stubble and a tiny lock of dark hair falling over one eyebrow, he could be a Prada ad. Also, if he were twenty years younger. His black Nikes made him look less hip. The rounded toes were all wrong. Their son was still at his playdate. The house would be very empty when her husband left. She squeezed him tightly, mashed her nose against his shirt, which somehow smelled of its color: light, light green. A medium green shirt would have been unthinkable. Might as well wear loafers without socks. Or take out a membership at the Reading Room on the path above the beach—the Reading Room, where the joke was that there wasn't a book in the entire place.

They disengaged. He raised a hand. She did the same. From under the bed, the cat poked out his head, then nearly flattened himself to crawl into the room. He walked in a half circle with his tail in the air, white tip flicking. They'd tied a bell to his collar, but the week before she'd found a dead bird in the yard.

She heard his footsteps on the stairs (or imagined them; they'd been newly carpeted), then the front door clicking shut. She waited to hear the garage door. Okay. She heard the car radio and the sound of gravel under the tires in the driveway, then only the wind that blew up. She went to the window and picked up the binoculars that sat there. She raised them to her eyes, already knowing how bright the pink of the sky would appear, how silver the bottoms of the tree leaves, pale as the underside of a turtle. A turtle some nasty boys flipped over so it would be incapacitated, as they laughed and pointed at its scaly legs clawing the air.

The cat startled her, brushing her leg. It was feeding time. A bit past it. "Feeling time," she murmured, then did a double take and corrected herself: "Feeding time. Yes." His eyes were all bright desire, but he wouldn't utter a sound. You sometimes heard it other times, but only the most silent of demands was made for the nightly meal. The cat would claw the banister and his bell collar would tinkle if the request wasn't promptly fulfilled.

Across the road was a scene she wouldn't have noticed if the cat's touch hadn't made her lower the binoculars from the sky: a doe and her fawn, the mother hovering as the lanky-legged baby led the way, eating something hanging below the low leaves of a bush. The pair was listening, listening, but the doe was listening more keenly. Oh, how sad is it I have to pump myself up with my own importance? she wondered.

Suddenly conscious of her earrings, dangling pearls, she touched them lightly to still them. She swiveled to see the empty room, the ocean-intense span of blue spread across the huge bed, the dresser mirror allowing her to see behind her to the pink sky darkening above whatever scene had been happening before that was now out of sight. Was September deer season? October?

Please let the plane not crash, she thought, going weak in the knees.

This was a habitual thought. More or less like prayer.

ENDLESS RAIN
INTO A PAPER CUP

It was July, Myrtis's favorite month since school days, when it would seem the summer still stretched before you, and your tennis shoes were just the right soiled color with your toenails poking up the canvas, and the water had warmed up enough that you could swim in the ocean—though now she lived inland; there was no nearby ocean—and the hummingbirds were busily sucking nectar from the bee balm (red was the only color in the garden). The Fourth of July! Strawberries ripened in July and bathing suits went on sale. She still bought a new one every year to wear in the steam room at the gym; she hadn't waded into the Atlantic in years, even on visits to Raleigh and Bettina. How she wished her daughter also saw summer as a magical time when the world overwhelmed you with its bounty, but Jocelyn seemed to notice little if anything about the environment in which she lived. She looked myopically at her friends, and from very close distance, they mirrored her expression of incomprehension or boredom, or they laughed about how ridiculous everything was, whether it be a buzzing bee or people working in a community garden. Her former husband's idea of happiness and harmony with nature had been gambling amid potted plants in Atlantic City casinos.

She called Raleigh, as she'd promised she would, when she got the results from her blood test. It was late enough at night that Bettina wouldn't even know she'd called. If she wanted real information about Jocelyn, her brother was a better bet than her sister-in-law, who didn't really understand young girls and therefore projected even more negativity onto them than was there—if such a thing was possible. Raleigh had met Jocelyn's teacher and pronounced her "very nice, quite intelligent." That opinion could be relied on, more or less, factoring in that Raleigh rarely expressed doubts until after the fact, and that he liked young women. He'd been as mystified as the next guy by women when he was young and dating, but now he seemed to think the mere sight of one was as lovely as seeing the first robin of spring. As far as she knew, he'd never strayed in his marriage to Bettina, but who ever knew about such things when few birds and even fewer people mated for life. He picked up on the second ring. She could envision the blinking red button on the phone—an odd phone that flashed but never rang—so that of course he would not know someone was calling unless he was sitting in his study.

"Good news?" he said. The phone must also somehow indicate the caller's identity.

"Inconclusive. I tested positive for antibodies to mono, so at some point I had it. It might have been a year ago when

THE STATE WE'RE IN

I thought I had flu. The test for Lyme came back okay, but something about it was borderline, and the doctor wants to repeat it in a couple of weeks. How's my girl? How are you, for that matter?"

"I'd say she's doing well. She's bored here, of course, but I think it's for the best. So would you say you're feeling less tired?"

"I slept from one until four. That's going to wreck my sleep tonight, but I was just so exhausted, I couldn't stay awake. All I did today was take the car in for an oil change."

He coughed softly, turning his head away from the phone. He said, "I came upon the key to Bettina's diary. She was out, so I read a few pages."

"She hid the key where you could find it?"

"In the bottom of the Excedrin bottle. Can you imagine? It was on a thin gold chain underneath the last of the pills. She must write in it when I go jogging."

"How I envy you being physically fit. Not everybody who has a metal plate in his leg would go running at your age. How are Jocelyn's essays? Does she put enough effort into them?"

"They seem to worry her a lot. She certainly doesn't like writing them. I was that way, myself, back in school. I don't think that young people like to be obliged to address subjects not of their own choosing."

"How are we going to get her to pass algebra? That's the big question."

Raleigh had gotten straight As in high school. It was how he'd gotten into West Point. His former running buddy, who'd recently relocated to Phoenix for the warmer winters, had been his classmate. He missed their twice-weekly runs. Though he'd told no one, there was some possibility he might need an operation on his leg. He was the one who'd bought the big bottle of Excedrin. Bettina had taken most of the pills. "One thing at a time," he said.

"What have you been doing other than being physically fit and being Jocelyn's uncle? We're all expected to be diverse in our interests and to give back. It's like we're all still trying to have a good résumé to get into college, whatever our age. Remember when I feigned interest in old ladies in nursing homes? Now I'm going to be one of them soon."

"Today I contributed nothing to any good cause and listened to 'Across the Universe.' The Beatles."

"I know who sang 'Across the Universe.'"

Bettina was right; sometimes his sister did sound very much like Jocelyn. He said, "Jocelyn might like to know you called."

"I'll call her in a day or so, when I'm not so headachy."

"Why should you have constant headaches? What do they say?"

"They don't answer questions like that. They do blood work."

"But I'd think that if you asked—"

"Ha!" she said. "You must have different experiences with those guys than I do. I suppose that's true. They take men more seriously. That, and you can continue to have your delusions about good communication because you don't ask questions of doctors or of anyone else, do you?"

"My training taught me to listen," he said. "But don't be ridiculous. Of course I ask questions."

"So you'll question Bettina about the diary?"

"No," he said, snorting softly. "That isn't at all likely."

"You'll secretly carry a grudge. That's what she says about you, you know. That when you're saying one thing, she can hear all the other things unsaid rolling around in your head like marbles, shooting off in all directions."

"We get along," he said, after a long pause.

Her tone softened. "I so much appreciate what you and Bettina are doing for Jocelyn. And I'm relieved that at least she's doing the work. Maybe it will give her more self-confidence when school starts in September."

"She's made some friends. I think things are okay," he said. He'd decided not to mention Jocelyn's new bangs, cut jaggedly on a sharp diagonal, or the pink streak in her hair, which he understood to be temporary. Who knew what his own daughter Charlotte Octavia's hair looked like, or whether she'd shaved her head? Her only overture in many months had been to send a pound of Kenyan coffee beans. It had been excellent coffee. About half the bag remained. He had suggested they store the remaining beans in the freezer, but she thought that unnecessary. In her diary, Bettina had called him prissy. How hugely insulting. It suggested, at least to him, homosexuality.

"I'll call again soon," Myrtis said. "I really am indebted."

"Nonsense," he said, as he hung up.

"Uncle Raleigh?"

He jumped. His eyes shot to the mirror hung beside the desk—the mirror whose border was patterned with little ducklings that had once hung in his daughter's bedroom, where they now stored clothes out of season and where Bettina had set up a little area with a rocker, to read her cook-books and to reread her beloved Edgar Allan Poe. One would certainly be a good antidote to the other, and Excedrin would not be required. Jocelyn stood in front of him in a volumi-nous T-shirt hanging over leggings (in July!). She was wearing socks over the tights and Hello Kitty slippers.

"Was that my mom?" she said.

"It was. Yes. Come in, Jocelyn. Sit down."

"Did she ask if I was doing all my homework? Did you give her a good report?"

"It wasn't a report, Jocelyn. We discussed the fact that you were working hard, yes. She's going to call back soon. Still doesn't have much energy. No one does, recovering from surgery."

The way his niece settled herself in a chair, plunking down with absolute resignation, and without any thought of a moment's pleasure, always surprised him. He suspected she came by his office so often to ask questions that were pointed and blunt, though perhaps not the issues that were most on her mind.

"Can you do me a favor, Uncle Raleigh?" she said. "Since you're an adult, can you maybe call the hospital and find out if one of my friends is there?"

"Which friend?" he said. "Who is that?"

"T. G.'s father's your friend, right? You didn't hear?"

"Hear what?"

"Well, like, he tried to commit suicide."

Charlotte Octavia had attempted to take her own life once. Twice, to be honest. Though they'd paid for psychia-trists, he'd never really understood why. He found the whole subject almost paralyzing. "Hank is my friend, yes," he said. "I can't believe T. G. would do a thing like that. It wasn't Nathaniel, you're sure?"

"Well, yeah. One person's T. G. and then there's his brother Nathaniel," she said. "It was T. G."

"When did you find out about this?"

"The other day, on the beach," she said. "If you call the hospital, they hear it in your voice you're young. I thought maybe you could find something out."

"My god, how absolutely terrible," he said, picking up his cell phone. "The last time I saw Hank or heard anything from him was playing golf last week." The phone was programmed with the number of the hospital. Also, the police. The surgeon he'd recently consulted about his leg. The butcher, the baker, the candlestick maker. No—none of them existed on his phone. As he'd entered the numbers, he'd dropped out so many names he felt he'd never call again; he didn't have to scroll down far to find anything. "Patient information," he said aloud. "Question," he said. Jocelyn was holding a Scünci in her teeth, unwinding her braid. A small strand of hair pinker than the rest revealed itself, just as a human being came on the phone. He asked about the condition of a patient named Thomas Grant Murrey. Jocelyn ran her fingers through her bangs and felt them flop lightly onto her forehead again. T. G. had liked her pink streak, but not the bangs. She was growing them out. "M-u-r-r-e-y, correct," her uncle said. "No, but if a family member is there, I'm a close friend of the boy's father," he said. He covered the mouthpiece. He whispered to Jocelyn, "Nobody's there. That's the good news and the bad news." He listened for another few seconds. T. G. had been admitted, but there were to be no phone calls to his room. When her uncle thanked the person and hung up, he said, "I don't know. You might be able to talk to him in the morning."

"Why do you think so?" she said.

It was a reasonable question. My god, what poor Hank Murrey must be going through right now. This was also sure to put Nathaniel into a worse tailspin, to say nothing of Hank's vain, high-strung wife, who acted like she lived with wild boars rather than with her husband and sons, lavishing all her attention on her only daughter. "Because in hospitals, they really believe in mornings," he said. "It's an old cliché, right? Everything might be better in the morning."

"You think I might be able to talk to him because of a cliché?"

At such times—when she seemed to echo what he'd said, yet she'd missed his point—he was never sure if she was mocking him, or whether she truly did not understand what he'd tried to say. Was she a little thickheaded, or was she just, of course she was *just*, an adolescent.

"I meant that hospitals trust that most situations change by morning," he said, a bit dully. She must be very upset about her friend. Why hadn't she told him immediately? He wished he had something better to offer. He also wished to avoid surgery on his leg. He wished Bettina did not keep a diary—especially one that was so critical of him. He supposed he might also wish for no one to ever go to bed hungry anywhere in the world and for peace.

"So, you and my dad. You drank together, right?"

Where did that come from? He said, "We'd have the occasional beer. The drinking problem was mine, not his."

"But you hung out together."

"Yes. We sometimes worked together."

"In a job you can't talk about because you had a security clearance, but my dad didn't."

"Your father didn't require a security clearance, no."

"So were you smarter than he was?"

"Brighter? Than your father? I had great respect for your father's intellect and perceptions. I went to military college, and he didn't. It made our outlooks somewhat different."

"But did you have the same outlook on girls?"

"What do you mean?" She was often very direct, though he suspected that most such questions were at some remove from what she really wanted to ask. She could certainly be just as difficult to talk to as Myrtis.

"I mean, did you pick up girls?"

"Before we were married? You're asking if we dated women? How would I have gotten to know your aunt if we'd never gone out?"

She shrugged.

"That was what you were asking?" he said.

"Well, not if it makes you mad."

"I'm not mad, I'm a little taken aback. True, I didn't expect such a question. But yes, he and I went on a few double dates together, before I introduced him to Myrtis. As things turned out, I was sorry that I introduced him to her, but if I hadn't, I suppose we wouldn't have you, and that would obviously be terrible."

"You say things to flatter me," she said. "Can I ask you one more question? How did you go from your big important job to selling cars?"

He frowned. What could she mean? What was underlying *that* question? "Cars?" he said, genuinely puzzled.

"Mom said you were a used car salesman."

"Then your mother was putting you on. I once had an office above a car dealership, but that's hardly—"

"If you weren't a salesman, then what were you?"

"It's nowhere near as interesting as you'd like to think—or maybe as I'd like to think—but it's not something I can talk about."

"I wish I had a security clearance. There's plenty of stuff I'd rather not talk about," Jocelyn said. "Uncle Raleigh, does my mom just not tell the truth, or do you think she was confused because of where your office was?"

"I assume she was being sarcastic," he said. "But I don't know."

"Whatever," Jocelyn said. "So you won't tell me what kind of women they were, either?"

"Tall and short. Educated and not. As your mother is fond of saying, the whole world is filled with people. If women came up to us in a bar, you could have a drink or a dance and not have sex, you know. It's only in the movies that men like your father and I have sex all the time." He might have said too much. "We might revisit this topic in a few years," he said.

"But, so, I don't get it about you and Aunt Bettina. She doesn't seem anything like you."

"At this age, people are nothing but their differences."

She pulled the toe of her tights and let it go. Dust streamed into the air. She said, "Can I just call you Raleigh? It makes me feel like a baby, having to always say 'Uncle.'"

"Fine with me," he said. "Let's continue this discussion in the morning, okay?"

"You're going to save Mom's house, right?"

"Please don't feel that your home is going to disappear. That's not going to happen, unless there's an earthquake or a sinkhole." He patted her ankle. "It's summer," he said. "What's with the tights?"

"I'm growing my leg hair, and it's at sort of an ugly stage."

"I see. Well, good night."

He was nothing like Bettina, Jocelyn thought. Bettina had given her mother different styles of Spanx for her birthday, which had been a total snark attack, and her mother hadn't even realized it.

"Words are flowing out like endless rain into a paper cup. They slither while they pass, they slip away across the universe," he half sang. " 'Across the Universe,' by the Beatles. A group from London who became famous and appeared on something called *The Ed Sullivan Show*."

"You're being retarded. You know I know who the Beatles are," she said, springing up, then looking back at him over her shoulder. Did any marriages make sense, or was he right about what he'd told her weeks ago, and there was a sort of use-by date stamped on them with an invisible watermark, like semen on the sheets?

In the parking lot outside the school, Jocelyn said to Ms. Nementhal, "I don't know why I did what I did the other night. I think I was just scared. Like you'd think I was involved in some way." What she was talking about was not saying hello, let alone

offering to drive Ms. Nementhal home after the boys threw
bottles from the car and broke the window of the pizza place.
It had sort of flipped her out to see Ms. Nementhal so rattled.

"Thank you for explaining," Ms. Nementhal said.

"It's not a very good explanation, I know. I don't know why
I do some of the things I do. It's like I caused some problem
when I didn't, but I don't think anybody will believe me."

"Of course it had nothing to do with you," Ms. Nementhal
said.

"I talked to my uncle, and he said you probably understood everybody was in a panic. I wanted to say something,
but I didn't know what to say."

"We all have limitations," Ms. Nementhal said.

"My mom's recovering from surgery, that's why I'm in
Maine. I could have taken an after-school course in Con-
cord to make up for my F in algebra, but my mom thought I
shouldn't be around after her surgery, so she sent me here,
to take your course, and live with my aunt and uncle."

"I see. I'm sorry about your mother. Will she be okay?"

"My aunt's a whack job. She had a biopsy that turned out
negative, but ever since she's shoveled in food twenty-four-
seven, which is what I was doing at the pizza place. I was picking something up for her. She has these constant requests
that we just, you know, try to do our best with. Like, at midnight she gets desperate for Neutrogena. Things like that."

"Neutrogena soap?"

"Right. Soap."

Ms. Nementhal nodded. She did not have annoying bangs
that flopped into her eyes. T. G. had said to her, "What's the
point of bangs, if the second you cut them, you start growing

them out?" Ms. Nementhal had said nothing in class about T. G.'s absence, but Jocelyn felt sure she knew what had happened. She watched her teacher's face for some sign of it, as they walked back toward the building.

"Is that guy Márquez still alive? You'd really like to meet him, right?"

"No, sadly. He died pretty recently, though. He was really a genius."

"My uncle tested genius in something," Jocelyn said. "Not that he thinks like Márquez."

Ms. Nementhal nodded again. She'd gone to her car to get her cardigan. The school was too highly air-conditioned, but there were signs at the windows saying not to open them.

"What are your interests, besides my course?" Ms. Nementhal said as they walked up the stairs. She probably knew that Jocelyn had no idea what the course was about until someone else enrolled her.

"Music? Beyoncé, and everything? I'd like to see the Grand Canyon. My uncle said he'd go with me when I graduated from high school. You can walk out over it on some glass platform, or whatever. It's all there, right below you."

"I'd be scared to death," Ms. Nementhal said. "Well, some of my other interests are tossing pots and French cooking, but I'm just learning about cooking. When I go to graduate school, I'm going to try to find a way to combine my interests in Egyptian art and poetry writing, and maybe I'll take a course in French literature."

Who would ever have thought Ms. Nementhal was anything but an overachiever? "Cool," Jocelyn said. "Where did you go to school?"

"Yale."

"That's really hard to get into, isn't it? Someone in the class is like dying to go to Yale."

"I suspect I know who that is."

Ms. Nementhal held open the side door. Jocelyn trotted ahead of her, her ears a little zingy, for some reason. Just listening to Ms. Nementhal had been exciting. She seemed to think she could do anything. If Jocelyn ever got into any college, it would be a miracle. Her mother said that tutoring for the SAT was too expensive, and she couldn't disagree. All you could do was read stuff on the Internet and get pointers from your friends, the most helpful so far being that the questions were essentially simple, but they pointed you in a direction that made you question your own perceptions, so you'd change things at the last second and answer wrong.

They were already in the classroom, so there was no time to ask Ms. Nementhal a final question. It would have been: if Magical Realism was in poems—as they'd learned that morning, for what seemed like five hours—why had she made them read so many passages from Márquez? The Charles Simic poems were fun and went zooming around your head in all directions as if they were hummingbirds.

When class let out, Angie caught up with Jocelyn, who'd just been texted by her mother on her iPhone: T. G. was being moved to McLean, some mental institution outside Boston. It was the same place where *Girl, Interrupted* took place—which was a book she'd read in the bathroom, because her mother refused to let her read it.

"Jocelyn—isn't that your aunt?" Angie said, looking up.

Oh, yes, it was: Bettina, coming their way, taking big

strides, her face absolutely without expression, which was weird and whacked.

"Hi, Aunt Bettina!" she called, but she felt as if someone else had shouted her name. She'd only said hello because her aunt would have felt dissed if she hadn't.

"We've been asked to preorder Girl Scout cookies, which really isn't the point of Girl Scout cookies," BLT said. She seemed a little out of breath. Why would her aunt have come to pick her up? Her mother always objected to people just jumping into a conversation. Bettina had not really greeted them and seemed to be very worked up. Was something wrong with her mother?

"Is everything okay?" Jocelyn said.

"I forgot your eye doctor appointment. I've got too much going on. We've got to hurry. It's in Kittery. Anna, how are you?" Bettina said to Angie. Jocelyn watched as Angie opened and closed her mouth, then said, "Fine, thank you."

"I suppose I should ask if we can drop you off, but we can't go out of our way," Bettina said to Angie. "Do you take the bus or walk?"

"Oh, thank you very much, but I like to walk home because it clears my mind and I can think about how I'll start writing the next assignment," Angie said, superpolitely.

"These assignments! You girls think about nothing else!"

Angie flashed her I'm-glad-we're-all-girls smile. She actually blew a kiss with her fingertips as she turned in the opposite direction. Her Toms shoes made of silver, sparkly material that looked like she'd stomped through Christmas tree tinsel were totally great. Jocelyn watched her go, envying her. When Angie got home, there would be fresh-baked cookies. They were from a roll of store-bought dough, but still: her mother tried.

"Aunt Bettina, is everything okay with my mom?"

"Well, she has Lyme disease, it turns out, so I can hardly say everything's fine. She called just a while ago. It's in an early stage, though, so let's hope she has a quick recovery."

"Lyme disease? OMG. We had a unit on that at school."

"Please use the English language and don't act like you're texting me," Bettina said. "We've discussed that before."

"Oh, shit! Poor Mom!"

"Could you favor me with a slightly more profound thought, do you think? Such as, 'What's the time frame for her to feel better?' or 'What should I do around the house to make things easier on Mom?'" She stopped and stared at Jocelyn. "And do you think you could stop acting like someone's trying to pass you a volleyball and walk at my side, so I don't have to shout? You are capable of walking in a straight line, I assume?"

"Aunt Bettina, you're always on my case!"

"Well, someone has to try to communicate with you. Your uncle's gone to California. At least, I think that was his intention before he got a phone call from that brother of your friend, Nathaniel, is it? who acts like T. G.'s condition is of no concern. His father went to McLean's today with his lawyer, and your father got a call, with what's his name—Nathaniel—whining that they were lacking a pitcher for their softball game. He thought your uncle should do it."

"I don't understand. He was going to California? Why?"

"Your uncle used to call these spur-of-the-moment trips his Magical Mystery Tours. He doesn't give very good explanations, you know that. But wait. I think he's taking that trip next week. Did he tell you about it?"

"No," Jocelyn said glumly. Adults were totally secretive. They wouldn't tell you the most interesting things, like about a trip somewhere, but they'd ask repeatedly how many washings were still to go before the color came out of your hair, and why you were wearing tights. A robin pulling a worm from the grass got Jocelyn's attention. It was obvious why Charlotte Octavia had broken off contact with her mother, but it seemed sad that she didn't have much of a relationship with her father, either. Try as she might, Jocelyn couldn't imagine Raleigh acting as aggressively as his wife.

Bettina had parked far away, though there were many closer parking places. When they got to the car, Bettina said, "You're on your own with those essays from now on. I've told Raleigh, he's off the hook. It's your future and you can figure out how to proceed. You aren't helped by his substituting one word for another."

"Aunt Bettina, excuse me, but Uncle Raleigh *makes me* show him my homework."

"Well, I personally think he might have gone to McLean with Hank Murrey and his lawyer, that's where he is, not pitching a softball game, I don't think." Bettina raised the cotton vest she was wearing to her face and blotted her forehead. Gross! Anybody knew not to do a thing like that. Her aunt was sweating. She did not turn on the ignition. Finally, talking more to herself than to Jocelyn, she said, "Okay, it's off to the eye doctor's."

"I didn't know about this appointment," Jocelyn said. Her aunt said nothing. She felt like she was in *Alice in Wonder-*

land. Nothing made much sense. Next, a white rabbit would appear, but until it did, she stared at the digital clock in the car. She thought if she focused her attention on something, she might not cry. Summer school was exhausting, T. G. was in a hospital somewhere she'd have no way to visit, and her mother had Lyme disease. Just great.

Parallel-parking, Bettina hit the curb with the back wheels, hard. "For Christ's sake," she said. "They build curbs now like they're soapboxes in Trafalgar Square, like we're supposed to stand there and rant about something. Just like my trip to England, which I suppose I'll never see again, it's so impossible to travel because they have to body-search everyone."

Oh, please let me live through this summer, Jocelyn thought, as she followed Bettina into the building. This was the eye doctor's? Why were they there? She sank into a chair and picked up *People* magazine, while Bettina charmed the receptionist, thanking her profusely for working her in, her sickly sweet smile at odds with her bizarre body language. The vest she was wearing made her look like she'd gotten tangled in a parachute. And she was sweating like she'd been doing Zumba. She stared at the magazine as her aunt took the clipboard from the receptionist and sat in a chair beside her to fill it out. She skimmed an article about Jennifer Aniston and her new fiancé. Good looking, in a conventional way. It would be so great to be Jen, with totally perfect hair and a flawless complexion and no Aunt Bettina in her life. So what if she'd lost Brad Pitt?

A man sitting in the waiting room got up and went to the watercooler, pulled a paper cup from the dispenser, and filled it quaveringly with cold water. He sipped. Jocelyn thought that he was aware that her aunt was in a state, he so deliberately avoided looking in their direction.

"Do you have allergies to medicine?" Bettina asked.

"Not that I know of," she muttered.

"What's your birthday?"

"Aunt Bettina, it's the same day as yours. We've had, like, ten joint birthday celebrations."

"Show some respect when you speak to me," Bettina said. At this, the man shot Jocelyn a sympathetic look. He picked up a copy of *Garden & Gun,* leaned back in the orange plastic chair, opened the magazine to the middle, and crossed his legs.

"Jocelyn?" the receptionist said. "And Dr. Miller? Sir, you'll be in the first room on the right, and Jocelyn, I'm happy to meet you, I'm Jenny, if you'll follow me."

Jocelyn stood and followed the receptionist and the other man through the door. In her peripheral vision, she saw her aunt draw a large *X* through an entire section of the form. She drew in a deep breath, then exhaled. "Jenny," she said. "My aunt's acting really strange. You've got to trust me on this. I've got to call my mother. Or no, I should call my uncle. I've got to call my uncle."

"Really?" Jenny said.

"Really. She was raving about Girl Scouts on the way over here. She was driving, like, crazy."

The toes of Jenny's black patent leather clogs touched each other. "She did seem a little upset when she called," she said. "What do you want me to do?"

"I don't want to intrude," Dr. Miller said, coming into the room, "but your mother is in a sweat and seems in some

81

distress." Where did *he* come from? He thought Aunt Bettina was her *mother?* She was totally not. Jenny seemed as surprised as Jocelyn that he'd simply walked into their room.

"What's the problem out there?" said a man in a white coat—though not the White Rabbit—coming into the room, frowning deeply.

"We should call an ambulance, I think," Dr. Miller said.

"That's what I thought," the tall man said. "How do you do," he said, suddenly, turning to Jocelyn. "I'm Dr. Baird. Are things not so good with your aunt?"

"I texted him from the waiting room," Dr. Miller said to Jocelyn. All of this was amazing. Somebody was going to do something. She couldn't believe her good luck.

"I've never seen her before today," Jenny said to no one in particular.

"Ambulance on the way," Dr. Baird said, dropping his iPhone back into his coat pocket. "And you are Ms.—"

"Jocelyn," Jocelyn said.

"Ms. Jocelyn," Dr. Baird said. "May I ask how old you are?"

"Seventeen," Jocelyn said. "I like to read with a magnifying lens, because it makes the print huge. I can see fine without it. I don't even wear glasses. She saw me reading with it the other night and—"

"Is your aunt your legal guardian?" Dr. Baird said, looking at her chart.

"No. I live with my mother."

"I see," Dr. Baird said. "Well, the ambulance will be here any minute. She'll be fine. Jenny, shouldn't we call Jocelyn's mother?"

"We have to call my uncle," Jocelyn said. "My mom's in

Massachusetts. She just had an operation, and she's got Lyme disease, too. She, like, totally couldn't do anything about this. She doesn't even know there *is* a magnifying lens."

"Okay, Jenny, can you help out here?" Dr. Baird said.

"She's secretive about everything. My aunt, I mean. Her own daughter doesn't speak to her, really. She keeps a diary and writes in it in the bathroom. She basically hates me."

Dr. Baird looked at Dr. Miller, who stood mutely in the doorway. "Fridays are always the worst," he said.

"Isn't that the truth," Dr. Miller said.

"It's all going to be fine," Jenny said. "Excuse me, and I'll . . ."

"Is your aunt diabetic?" Dr. Miller asked.

"I don't think so."

"Do you think we might look in her handbag?" Dr. Miller said to Jocelyn.

"I don't care," she said.

Jenny exited and came back holding her aunt's purse by one strap. It bulged open. On the first rummage, she brought out a bottle of pills and handed them to Dr. Baird.

"You called it, Ed," Dr. Baird said to Dr. Miller.

"Did she, like, see you taking her purse?" Jocelyn asked.

"She's having a little rest in her chair," Jenny said. She could match Angie for false brightness any day.

"I don't have any money and I don't know how to get home," Jocelyn said.

"No worries!" Jenny said. "Isn't that right, Dr. Baird? Trina's off at four o'clock. She can give you a lift, Jocelyn. Or I can."

"You could ride in the ambulance with your aunt to the hospital?" Dr. Baird hinted.

"I'm afraid of her," Jocelyn said.

"Trina will take you home," Jenny repeated.

"Your uncle? Do you know where he is?" Dr. Baird said.

"Maybe pitching a softball game, or maybe at a mental hospital?"

"He might be at a mental hospital?"

"A friend of mine tried to kill himself," Jocelyn said.

"Unbelievable," Dr. Baird said. "Have we tried to get in touch—"

"He didn't answer his phone," Jenny said to Dr. Baird.

A red, rotating light on the ceiling let them know the ambulance had arrived without its siren. Dr. Baird excused himself and went to the waiting room. He certainly did not move at White Rabbit speed. Once, playing field hockey, her friend Rachel had tripped on a big rock and broken her ankle. The bone had been sticking out of her foot and there had been blood everywhere when the ambulance arrived. Jocelyn had tried to comfort her by holding her hand and telling her to close her eyes. Which was more than she'd done for Bettina—although Bettina only gave orders, she never listened to anything.

When the ambulance left and she left with Trina, carrying her aunt's handbag, no one had heard back from Raleigh.

"You want to know how crazy things can get?" Trina said, starting her car and pulling on her seat belt. Trina had bright blue, squared-off fingernails, which were totally awesome. She was even cooler than Jenny, and Jenny was pretty cool. "Okay, so you tell me where I turn off Route One," Trina said. "I know York pretty well. One of my friends was there with her boyfriend. Some rich guy didn't want him to be found because he didn't want him to be deposed, okay? So they put him in a rental house, and here's where it turns into a modern-day horror story." *Beep beep.* "Damn! Did you hear that? The car keeps unlocking itself. Why would it do that? Like I was saying, though, it's not exactly Stephen King, but still. You know what the bad guys did? They put yellow jacket nests into the ground, like they were planting flower seeds, because he was way allergic to yellow jacket stings. Aha. So first they relocated the guy, then they had these yellow jackets kill him."

"Nests in the ground? How do you do that?"

"It's like I said, you put them in like marigold seeds, or something."

"No way."

"After he died, my friend—the one he was living with? She found out that he'd committed a really bizarre crime in another state. She'd been engaged to him! He might have done the same thing to her. When he died, her parents got her to a shrink. She got something called hysterical blindness, which means you lose your sight but nothing's wrong with you. It's a conversion disorder. Besides this, it turns out she's pregnant with the guy's kid! About the blindness thing, the shrink called Dr. Baird, because he'd been her doctor, right? I'm sure whatever Dr. Baird did was totally correct, because he's totally a professional. I wouldn't mind being married to Dr. Baird and having a million dollars. Anyway, my friend's doing better and she was even lucky enough to have a miscarriage. Her e-mails aren't censored anymore, so it all worked out, right?"

"It sounds pretty fucked up," Jocelyn said.

"Well, you have to be really careful of everybody you meet for a really long time. And even then, they lie to you." Trina reached between the seats and pulled something out of a box. "You can blow these up and pretend they're cow udders," she said, holding a latex glove to her lips and blowing into it.

Jocelyn burst into laughter, then clamped her hand over her mouth.

"Okay, let me pull over here. Okay, it's a text from Dr. Baird that your uncle called and he's on his way to the hospital. See? It's all working out."

"I'm really glad he's not in California," Jocelyn said.

"I'd totally love to live there, but it would take me farther away from Dr. Baird," Trina said. "He came with me on his lunch hour and helped me figure out financing for my car. He gave me a raise at Christmas. I haven't had a roommate for a year. It's totally awesome that I go home and do whatever I want."

"What things do you do?"

Beep beep.

"A for instance? I defrost marinara sauce and eat it with a spoon, no pasta."

"Does it matter that the car keeps locking and unlocking?" Jocelyn said.

"It's got a mind of its own. That, or it's auditioning to be the Road Runner."

Jocelyn smiled. "My mother loves pasta. She'd want your marinara sauce with linguini," Jocelyn said.

"Okay, so the thing is, you want it, you can have it, but you want to eat sauce with a spoon, that's cool too, you know?"

Jocelyn nodded. Somehow, she didn't feel convinced

she'd ever see her mother again—that was the unformed thought that she'd kept in her head like a headache for hours, though now it exploded like a jack-in-the-box. Oh, her old toy box, filled with what her mother called "my eBay nest egg for old age." It was on a shelf in the closet and she hardly ever thought about any of the things in it anymore. Since Trina had gotten the text message, though, she did believe she'd see Raleigh. Would he be mad at her for not going with Bettina? Her aunt's purse felt like a boulder in her lap. Jenny and Trina were nice. She thought she'd like to be a working woman like them—they were way cooler than Ms. Nementhal—though Dr. Baird certainly wasn't her type.

"What's the story with living with your aunt and uncle?" Trina said. She turned on the radio, so whatever Jocelyn said was sure to be partially drowned out by heavy metal.

"My mom had a hysterectomy, so she sent me here for the summer," Jocelyn said.

"She did? That's no big whoop anymore. I bet they sucked out her uterus using a laparoscope instead of cutting an incision. She'll be fine."

"Yeah," Jocelyn said.

"She can wear her bikini again!" Trina said.

Jocelyn looked at her.

"Are you an only?"

"What?"

"Only child."

"Oh. Yeah."

"I thought so. So am I. Only children are really bright and sensitive, you know? I'd be totally perfect for Dr. Baird, if he only realized it. Ha!"

"You've really got a crush on him," Jocelyn said.

"Well, *yeah*," Trina said. "But his wife's this Harvard graduate, and they already have three kids and a Labradoodle. Before they ended the space program, she grew up wanting to be an astronaut."

"Were you kidding about the bees?" Jocelyn said. "You turn at the light. Left."

Trina put on her directional signal. "Bees?" she said.

"Yeah. That killed that guy."

"Yellow jackets, not bees. No, it's true, he died. He was a freak, though. I don't know how she hooked up with him. A freak can't keep it hidden, I don't think. Though there was that guy who cut people's lawns and was really a mass murderer."

"What?"

"BTK. Bind, torture, kill, I think it was. He was married! She divorced him!"

She'd heard something about that, but she tried not to think about such things. There'd also been the guy who lived in his car and thought his dog was telling him to kill people. She'd found out about him reading one of Zelda's graphic novels. Trina would probably know exactly who that guy had been. She would also have seen the 3-D *Planet of the Apes*. Of course she would have. And asked for extra butter on her popcorn. Trina seemed to be in her late twenties, maybe early thirties. By the time she herself was thirty, she hoped to have the courage to ask for butter anytime she wanted it—more butter, and more butter. Bettina, who was huge, put little dabs of butter on their corn with a tiny knife, as if she were cleaning someone else's ear with a Q-tip.

They were almost to the house. Two people in a silvery blue Solara convertible passed by, and Trina gave them the thumbs-up. The world belonged to Trina. Which was better than it belonging to her uncle or Bettina. Her mother, of course, wasn't even in the running. Her mother would be happy if her own life was a constant time-out—she wouldn't consider such a thing punishment if she could sit in a chair and not speak and not move and, most of all, not check her phone. She loved turning it off. Then the bill collectors went to voice mail and her daughter couldn't ask for anything and Raleigh wouldn't always be checking up on her. Raleigh. She was very glad he was still in Maine, instead of California. He'd told her a story recently and sworn her to secrecy. It was that her father, back when he still wanted to impress his wife, sometimes came back from a fishing trip with lots of trout he hadn't really caught. He'd bought them at the fish market. One time her mother had said, "Why are these so cold?" and he'd supposedly said to Jocelyn, "Remember this all your life, my little one. Your mother thinks that fish swim in warm water."

DUFF'S DONE ENOUGH

Duff Moulton changed his nickname from Chip to Duff when the old block he was supposedly chipped from died at age 103. Mrs. Terhune, who had no nickname, and whose first name was rarely spoken, had supplied him with homemade soup and oyster crackers over the last few years, receiving a handsome check from Duff's cousin at the beginning of each month for her efforts. She was seventy-four and quite able to continue making soup and doing everything else she was doing, thank you very much. She said this in response to a kindly phrased note that had come recently with one of the checks, Duff's cousin politely inquiring whether—especially considering the very bad winter they'd endured—it was too much for her to go to Duff's every day.

She understood that Chip was now to be called Duff, but he was eighty-two, and changing your name that late in life was ridiculous, so she either called him "my fine neighbor" or did not address him directly, relying on the

Maine "ey-ah," said rather loudly to let him know she'd entered his house.

It was big of her, she thought. Thirty-some years before, Chip's brother had led her on, then married a young Portuguese woman and moved away to Providence. Such things had happened to many of her women friends, the most notable being her friend Rochelle Pennybaker, whose ex-husband wooed her back over several years, remarrying her with a justice of the peace presiding and their twin sons present. (One came from Arizona and was thrilled; the other—a psychology researcher at Harvard—begged his mother to reconsider and also told his father to join AA. He didn't have much credibility, however, because he himself had been twice divorced.) Shortly after the honeymoon (heard this one before?) he did, indeed, join AA, where he took up with a transgender person—a lawyer, who managed to get the second marriage annulled. You don't think things like this happen in woodsy Maine, off the beaten path? It sounds more like L.A.? In Maine, there may be a path, but it's never clear, except perhaps to that great GPS programmer in the sky, and there are also significant numbers of beatings between husbands and wives, daughters and mothers, cousins and nephews—many of whom end up at the hospital ER, where I work. One came in last week with a Swiss Army knife sticking through his calf, bleeding profusely, in terrible pain, and all he could say over and over was that the person who stabbed him—who was standing right there, clutching his hand—was his cousin (female!).

Mrs. Terhune is a lady. I've rented her converted garage for the last six years or so, working on the novel I began in Iowa City, which I could summarize, but every day I live in fear that someone might have had the idea to publish a book on the same subject. To support myself, I work weekends as a sort of glorified janitor at the local hospital, and in the summertime at the local hardware store, which has a beautiful array of plants for sale. In winter I bartend three nights a week at one of the inns, which also assures me free cheese cubes. Mrs. Terhune is generous about giving me a container of soup or, when she makes it, because I really love it, tapioca. Inside my little house is a flat-screen, a Bose sound system (the outlet is in Kittery), and under grow lights, flourishing plants that would have otherwise died when they were unsold at the end of the season.

I began this story talking about Chip, now Duff. He's a rather overwhelming presence because he has hearing problems and talks loudly, but also because of his height, six four, and a lifetime of overcompensating for a strawberry stain over his forehead that dips down across his eyebrow. People notice him coming—that is what he often says when he doesn't know what else to say about some odd encounter he's had on one of his trips about town. He drives only in daylight, and only if he feels rested and clearheaded. I've learned that with old people, you have to listen to all their rationalizations: they go over and over their I'm-safe-because-I-say-I-am routines.

For the last year or so, since my book is about two-thirds finished, I've sometimes read aloud to Mrs. Terhune. Let me just say that Shackleton figures in the plot, and that like many people I've been fascinated by the doomed expedition and writers' various perspectives on it. It turned out that Mrs. Terhune had never heard of Shackleton or his expedition, and she became morbidly obsessed (as who isn't). She's probably heard fifty or sixty pages of the manuscript by now, and—this is so true of nonwriters—she always says that she can't understand why my whole book isn't about Shackleton. She can't get enough of frozen toes and sacrificed dogs.

One night in March when it was still unusually cold she brought Duff along with her for reading night. I have electric baseboard heat (expensive!). Duff has a furnace that doesn't work well; also, he's a New Englander, and cheap, so he won't turn up the thermostat. There the two of them were at my door, she with a jar of soup she'd made from tomatoes she'd canned, he just standing there, pretending to be chewing tobacco when he wasn't, his big boots caked with mud and snow. I did ask him to leave them outside. He hung on to Mrs. Terhune and to me, though I proved more useful in bending down and unlacing the boots and pulling them off, with his hand that wasn't on Mrs. Terhune's shoulder clutching my door frame. I don't even remember how I segued, that evening, from Shackleton to Bruce Chatwin's *In Patagonia*—probably because of the quality of his prose, which I much admire—only to learn, at the end of my little reading, during which we all sipped herbal tea with honey, that Duff's father had been to Patagonia. He'd also been to the Galápagos, and to the Suez Canal, where he'd gotten dengue fever. "He was no businessman, he was OSS, then CIA," Duff announced. "You might wonder, well, what's our business in the Galápagos? And the answer's mine to give. The tortoises. At one time, believe it or not, our country considered rigging up tortoises to record conversation going on around them. Well, you might ask: how many bad guys were going to step outside to talk important business, like the Galápagos was just one big backyard? The answer was—at least if you got them to the Galápagos—quite a number! There was some 'Go to the Galápagos' campaign after World War Two. That's where they wanted everybody to go, though most people preferred San Michael of Allende. You think about recent times and those boys, Nixon I think it was, trying to give Fidel Castro an exploding cigar. That's no joke."

I nodded. It was Kennedy, but it seemed like something Nixon would do.

"That was their best thought!" Duff said, loudly. "So a bunch of turtles . . . I mean, tortoises. My father taught me the distinction: tortoises. What I'm saying is, there was a big conference in the Galápagos, and they were sleeping in the sun or crawling their ten inches a day, or standing up, looking left and right, and plopping down again, wired for sound!"

"My fine neighbor, you are full of surprises," Mrs. Terhune said.

"That writer fellow, he happened to be an acquaintance of my father. You might ask, where would my father encounter the dashing Bruce Chatwin? Well, it was on faraway soil, where his Sherpa knew the Sherpa who was taking some Brits on a hike, and they thought in their Sherpa way that maybe they could lead the two expeditions together. One of the hikers was an English writer, name of Chatwin. When he and my father met, he was astonished at my father's age. Said he didn't look a day over sixty. Had some reluctance about letting the Sherpas get off easy, but they did agree they'd join up. But on the second day one of the men fell ill and had to be airlifted out with a ruptured appendix, so First Sherpa went ahead. Anyway, that first night, my father talked old age and dengue fever and London bars with Bruce Chatwin, who fell ill himself in the 1980s, but by then my father didn't read the paper, and except for reading *In Patagonia*, I don't think he ever read another of his books. I can't be sure of that. Anyway, my father—as you surely remember, Muriel— was always fired up about something or somebody, and for a while it was nothing but Chatwin, Chatwin, Chatwin. When he died, I wrote a note to Mrs. Chatwin, telling her how much that one meeting meant to my father and saying that if she remembered ever hearing about a Charles Manley Arthur Bromwell, that was my late father, who died at the age of one hundred and three."

Mrs. Terhune turned to me, the fingers of her free hand rubbing the warm mug. She said, "One time Mr. Bromwell was all fired up about digging a new well, and he had a dowser come, a famous one, who charged by the day. He looked and he looked. He couldn't find anything. So another dowser was called in, and bingo! He knew where to drill, but on drilling day, who should show up but Dowser Number One, who stood there disagreeing with where the dig should begin. He'd had a dream that he woke up from with tingling fingertips, he said, which had happened to him ten times previously, and every single time he'd been right: he'd envisioned the property in his dreams, and his fingertips had started to tingle, so that when he sat up in bed, he was pointing toward some part of the scene that remained as clear to him as if he were watching a movie. Then he'd sort of sleepwalk toward it—a gulley or a shaded area under oak trees—and his fingertips would turn hot and stop having that funny feeling, but when the digging began, it was always the right place." She turned toward Duff Moulton. "So, Chip—I mean, Duff: your late father, I believe he came up with the solution of not having either of the dowsers work for him, because he thought the man with the itchy fingers was clearly crazy, yet he'd cast enough doubt that he didn't want the other guy doing the work, either. When the well ran dry, someone else in the family called in the person who drilled a new one, so a well did get drilled successfully while Mr. Bromwell was still with us."

"If you don't think it's too forward of me, Mr. Moulton, how is it that your father was named Bromwell, and you Moulton?" I asked.

"Not forward, at all! Don't they complain that young people never ask questions? I was the first and last baby born to my parents, and my mother could never have another because they had to remove her inner workings when I was born. She was so sad, she cried for days, and finally my father said, "Well, why not name him for your side of the family, since we don't want the Moultons to die out." He cleared his throat and pretended to switch the tobacco plug from one cheek to the other. "That was a little joke. The Moultons aren't about to die out. Not before the Smiths do, anyway. All of that might take another meteor. But anyway, he was an enlightened man, or at least an unusual one. He'd get a gold medal now from the women's liberation front."

I looked at Mrs. Terhune. I suspected I shouldn't correct him and say he shouldn't say "front." I don't know why I bothered to send her a silent look, because she wasn't the kind of woman to return another woman's glance, and if a man looked at her for agreement, she'd only squint.

So that was more or less my evening with my landlady and the neighbor. Enough information was revealed to provide me with material for several books. Anyone prudent would have asked if they'd mind being recorded, but it wasn't until the next day that this possibility hit me, and then—in spite of being a bit shy—I went first to Mr. Moulton and asked, calling what he'd provide "an essential oral history," and also flattering him—I hoped I wasn't frightening him—about using his stories in my writing, someday. I figured that if I went to him first, Mrs. Terhune might also agree, but I missed my guess. "You go ahead and put your recorder in my fine neighbor's house, if he agrees, but I don't hold with wiring turtles or setting up a machine to talk into every time a thought pops into my head. No, I wouldn't want to sit around and do that. Most things are best forgotten. With that Shackleton man, you've got enough information to write for a lifetime! You go ahead and record Chip, I mean Duff, but Duff's done enough. You'll have to excuse me for saying no."

Mrs. Terhune—in fact, everyone in New England—was unwilling to rethink anything, so that was that. I thanked her and made plans to proceed with Duff (as he asked me to call him). I drove to Radio Shack to see what I could buy to make the recordings. I wanted something a little old-fashioned so it wouldn't put him off. In the back, they found a machine that took cassettes, of which they had a plentiful supply. The salesman, who looked about sixteen, was amazed at what the older salesman had managed to put his hands on. He examined all of it as if it were dinosaur dung. I drove home so excited; I could hardly believe what I'd stumbled into. This was the expedition that would go right. The dogs (that would be me) would prance forward effortlessly, devoted to their task. Soon we'd glide through to beautiful spring weather, day after day, until we arrived at our destination. Of course, I suspected that my unstated goal was to stop writing my book. That something about Duff and the new project was subversive, as well as extraneous. I almost had a first draft, and as any writer knows, once you have that the going gets easier. Then it's just editing: adjusting, adding the better word here and there, finding the perfect phrase, the enlightening metaphor, taking away the drift of words that have become too plentiful on the snowy white page. The new book might be better—much better—but it was a distraction from my story, the one I'd been moving forward with for years, in self-imposed near isolation, with only a radio to bring in Mozart to brighten the dark days.

Fate fooled me. Duff moved in with Mrs. Terhune, and together they agreed that I should finish the book I was writing and maybe, maybe we'd talk later, if summer wasn't too busy. He did not romantically move in with Mrs. Terhune. He did the sensible, New England thing of doubling up. He'd turn off the heat in his house and drain the pipes, and together they'd adequately heat her house, and split the bill. It was as if they'd just been waiting to be better friends and I'd facilitated it by being the hostess of an evening on which they got to know each other better. Duff moved into her back bedroom, the one with the toile de Jouy wallpaper that had been brought back by one of her mother's friends from her trip of a lifetime (sailing to Le Havre, France), the overall pattern repeating its story of Dutch people in dirndls and bonnets tied under their chins, walking along in their wooden shoes, tending their animals, swinging milk pails as they stroll past windmills.

The whole world's full of stories. I never doubted that. Every writer will tell you the same thing: it's next to impossible to find the inevitable story, because so many needles appear in so many haystacks. Most writers spend their entire careers—those who are lucky enough to have them—considering endless piles of hay, praying, just praying that a needle will prick their finger.

I suppose it pricked mine when I opened my door and saw Mrs. Terhune standing there with Duff Moulton. The union radiated inevitability, though I'm sure it was more apparent to me than to them. I was the spinner of tales whose closed-off world had been pricked like a big bubble. As with any accident—because accidents are by definition unexpected—you react instantly to that unmistakable, tiny stab of pain, so you rub your finger on your pant leg or you suck it for a second. It's a tiny, split-second annoyance unless it's bleeding all over everything, and you're embarrassed when people see that you've been hurt, so you insist that you haven't been.

ELVIS IS AHEAD OF US

The house at the end of our dead-end street had been for sale almost a year when two girls and a boy broke into it through the back bathroom window. They were kids from the neighborhood: Genevieve, Blake, and Ted. Genevieve and Blake were unlikely friends, Blake tall and lively, with ear piercings and blue fingernails, Genevieve very pulled together, more French than her mother born in Avignon (which her daughter had never seen and Mrs. DuPenn did not remember). Genevieve was always called Genevieve, though Blake was sometimes called Fuzzy. Ted was really Edward.

Barbara Gillicut, the Re/Max agent who had the listing of what the neighborhood kids called "the abandoned house," posted no photographs online except of the exterior. There was never an open house, and no one from the neighborhood asked for an appointment to view it, and for a while after the owner left, there was no word of its contents. Who knows why kids would get obsessed with something as ordinary as an empty house. But they did. They began to gather there in the evening and to peek in the windows, though they didn't see much of what was inside until they finally broke in and went into the room at the back, the one without windows.

Jon Enders, the owner, had seemed pleasant enough when he first bought the house—but that means next to nothing nowadays, I suppose. He hadn't exactly thrown a neighborhood barbecue, but when I dropped by with a paper plate of brownies he invited me in and we sat in the front room, which was beautifully arranged, though very spare: two chairs (two!) facing each other, each upholstered in a slightly different shade of blue velvet, and an enormous coffee table with a few stones on it, along with orchids whose budding stems were staked with chopsticks, and fashion magazines from foreign countries. Not all were fashion magazines. I went home with a borrowed *Paris Review*, which I found most enjoyable. Years ago, I'd worked at Le Pli salon in Cambridge, Massachusetts, coloring hair. Several models from the same agency often came in to get their hair foiled on the same day. One had lived in Paris in her teens and brought me madeleines. Another, an American girl from the South, brought me the best peanuts I'd ever tasted, which changed my mind about that nut. I don't think the other ever brought me anything, but like her friends, she was nice and tipped big.

If Jon had visitors, they were few, though in the summer months I saw stylish cars go to the end of the street, and once I was curious enough to step out to see if the silver Miata was parked in Jon's driveway again (it was), but beyond that it wasn't a socializing sort of neighborhood—which was why I thought the custom in our town of teasing newcomers into having a barbecue, then never reciprocating, was pretty mean. "Trial by fire!" my husband said. "Get it? It's a pun: the 'fire' of the barbecue." He was always pleased when he made a pun.

The first time the kids broke into the house, Genevieve told her mother about it later, because she told her mother everything. I was visiting Marie when Genevieve made her confession—perhaps thinking I'd be protection of some kind, and that her mother wouldn't scold her in front of a visitor. She reported that there was a mysterious door locked with a padlock. The dining room didn't even have a table, just a stand with a vase on it, and upstairs in one of the bedrooms there was a rowing machine and a set of free weights and a stationary bicycle and a flat-screen TV mounted on the wall. There was a bed and a bedside table in the other bedroom, nothing else. The bed was covered in what Genevieve described as some "elaborate quilted sort of Indian patterned thing, with little mirrors and all, and knots that looked like raspberries. Mostly silver and gray." I listened with interest, because Jon had not offered me a tour of the house the time I visited. Genevieve said that there was also a chair in the up-stairs hallway that she didn't see at first because it was a ghost chair—one of those stylish chairs you can see right through. But the strangest thing—and here she became quite excited, in that young-girl way she has that's going to charm boys forever . . . she said the shower curtain was the worst-looking thing she'd ever seen, printed all over with neon signs in re-ally bright paint, made to look like they were glowing. VIVA LAS VEGAS! appeared in green, orange, red—every possible color. When she left the room, Marie DuPenn rolled her eyes and said, "At least we can be thankful there wasn't some woman chained to the wall who had to give the owner blow jobs or be electrocuted."

When my husband got back from work I told him what I'd heard, and all he had to say was that in this day and age, he didn't understand why people didn't install sliding doors on their bathtubs. Our tubs had been replaced with shower stalls tiled in restful colors, the upstairs one with flooring called River Rocks.

"You have to admit that he was strange," I said, "hardly furnishing his house and nobody ever seeing him in the yard all the time he lived here."

My husband lived to refute me: "The guy figured out he'd bought a house in a boring town and he got out." Also, it was "Mrs. DuPenn's job to deal with her daughter's information, not ours." He tended to speak of people in the neighborhood formally—a habit he'd acquired being a lawyer.

To be honest, I didn't think the kids would break in a second time, though I was wrong. This had often been the case with our own son—my misguessing. Caleb was now making a fortune in Silicon Valley, driving a Beamer convertible, and engaged to an extremely interesting girl, a biologist who'd graduated from Harvard. One of the things I hadn't thought Caleb would do, years ago, was act on his intense hatred of the local high school, let alone blow up the toilet in the teachers' bathroom. Also, I hadn't expected that when he had a teenage crush on a tourist, he'd hitchhike to Colorado to see her—or that had been his intention until the police picked him up. I could give other examples of him just being a boy, but since his life has worked out fine, best to forget—including what he did to the leftover anatomy lab frogs.

When they broke in the second time, Ted, Genevieve, and Blake tried to be as quiet as possible, but Rollins the dog—who lived in the house next door to Jon Enders's—saw them and began barking and wouldn't stop, which drew my attention to what might be happening. Sure enough, when I walked a little way down the road I could see that the door was wide open. There was no light when I entered the house, just Ted shining his flashlight around the walls, and Blake running into the beam of light whenever she could, pretending that Ted was trying to put her in the spotlight. Once I stepped inside, he turned off the flashlight pretty quickly, and that left whatever moonlight seeped though the door and windows. For a split second it was my impulse to turn and run. I thought I'd walked into some Jeffrey Dahmer ghoulishness. Somehow, they'd pried open the padlocked door and heads were everywhere, though the lampshades put them into some perspective. "You came! You came!" Genevieve said, once they'd gotten over their fear that I was the police. Closer inspection (Ted leading the way) revealed what I'd seen to be busts of Elvis, arranged every which way on metal tables—the long kind that people use outside for buffets. Some were chipped, missing a chunk of nose, or a bit of white showing through pink lips. Hardly any depiction seemed exactly right, though as they circled and examined the lamp bases they instantly started a game, as Ted's flashlight danced over them: Find the Best Elvis. There would be a scratched cornea, just when Blake thought she'd won, or Genevieve would point out a missing black curl behind an ear. The lamp bases were about three feet high, minus their shades: Elvis in sunglasses; Elvis wearing a high white ruffled collar; Elvis with glitter on his cheekbones; Elvis with super-long eyelashes, a mascara fanatic's dream.

They began snapping pictures with their cell phones. Elvis made his way across the universe in seconds. He went (OMG!) to girls in boarding school and to Blake's half brother in Austin; he appeared in selfies with Ted, who tousled his own longish hair and did a pretty credible job of imitating Elvis's expression before relaying it to his basketball coach. The kids mugged and held their fingers up behind Elvis's head. They grouped some duplicate busts together and took turns crouching behind them, intruding their own faces into the lineup for the photograph. They thought all the Elvises were awesome. What did it mean? Genevieve wanted to know. Genevieve was pictured kissing him on his pink plaster lips. She ran home and got her mother, who was at first really perturbed to know she'd crept out of bed and broken into the house again, but by the time Mr. DuPenn got there, damp from the shower, his wife was walking around the tables with me, *mon dieu*–ing. "You put all these back the way they were," her husband said to Ted, trying to sound stern.

"What do you think they're all doing here, was he some big Elvis fan or something, I guess?" Ted said.

"I don't think they'd be here otherwise," I said.

"Oh no, this is wrong of us to be here," Marie DuPenn said. "We must go!"

"Come on, enough of this nonsense. It's after midnight," my husband said.

Blake wouldn't budge. She said it was the most amazing

thing she'd ever seen, even better than the first field of fire-flies she ever saw. She stroked one Elvis's brow, her fingers lingering on his dark brown curls.

"That guy got really fat out in Vegas," Ted said to me. "They had to like sew him into his costumes like trussing a turkey, and I think he popped out one time. Yeah." My husband asserted again that we had to get moving. Already, there were responses to the photos: a smiley face icon made out of a colon and close parenthesis; OMG LOL; xxURnutsxxband-supercul!:)huuuunh?

Nobody had to walk more than a few blocks home. The kids left by the front door, Blake grudgingly, Ted with a lot of bravado. As he tried to close the front door tightly, the top hinge came out of the doorjamb, and Ted said, "Bummer!"

My husband doubled back to inspect the problem. "Oh, hell, now I feel like it's my responsibility to fix the door," my husband said. "Is everybody satisfied now? You're going to be my assistant tomorrow, Ted, and we'll get that room pad-locked again while we're at it."

"Yo, world, the King is back!" Ted hollered, hardly worried about what he'd done, pumping his fist in the air. "Long live the King!"

"Shut up, Ted, you are so rude!" Blake said, kicking some pebbles aside.

"Hey, we could sell them on eBay and make enough money to go see an Elvis impostor in Vegas!" Ted said. He was quite keyed up. "All the food's free in the casinos. One of them just kicked out Ben Affleck for like forever, because he was mem-orizing the cards played, or something. He won hundreds of thousands of dollars. I read about it in the doctor's office."

"I'm surrounded by morons," Blake whispered harshly, seeming to be speaking to the moon. She looked over her shoulder at us, then picked up her pace and jogged toward home, head averted, hands clasped in loose fists in front of her.

I was just glad they were basically good kids. And I was glad, too, that there hadn't been a refrigerator full of decapitated heads. It was so harmless—someone's collection of Elvis lamps. Who wasn't eccentric? This was really a modest collection, considering some of the things people amassed: Nazi helmets; pictures of freaks; old dental instruments.

"Mr. Duncan, that guy was gay!" Ted said.

"Well, what if he was?" my husband said.

"Gay!" Ted repeated. "Blake didn't even get it that he was gay!"

My husband looked at Ted. I could almost hear him thinking, though I couldn't read his mind. Finally, he said, "It certainly was something to see."

"I've got to take really good photographs with my Nikon, Mr. Duncan," Ted said. "Also, we didn't search the cellar. Do you think there might have been real bodies down there?"

"Don't be ridiculous," my husband said. He turned to me, gesturing toward the Magerdons' side yard. Andrea Magerdon was getting chemo in New York. We'd heard she was doing fine, but she wouldn't be back until August. "Look at how well that trumpet vine's growing," he said. "Mine can't even find the post."

The following morning, though my husband left Ted two messages, he went back to the house alone to make the repairs, pretending to be more put out than he was. I walked partway with him, carrying a plastic gallon jug of water. The trumpet vine had been doing okay on its own, but the least I could do was pour some water on it, since the Magerdons obviously couldn't. A month earlier I'd thought of watering what remained of their garden, but the water had been turned off.

Who should my husband run into, of course (I saw this from afar, and was glad I hadn't accompanied him), but Barbara Gillicut, just starting up the walkway. "Hey, ho!" he called. "Barbara, please, a word."

He told me later that she had not been at all amused. Clients were coming in fifteen minutes, and what were they going to see but a busted front door? He assured her that it wasn't really damaged, and that he could fix it in five minutes. He gave her the usual talk about how kids will be kids, but these were actually pretty good kids. She disputed this, but he did discourage her from phoning Ted's parents. "Ted and Genevieve and Blake!" he said to her. "What do you bet they all end up successful or famous or both, and we look back on this as their little misadventure, which is absolutely nothing compared to all the kids burning down buildings and beating up street people and torturing rabbits. Barbara, please!"

He fixed the door. He was gone before the people arrived. When my husband returned to the house, he told me that Barbara Gillicut had said that she'd only recently undone the lock herself. Usually she asked people to remove memorabilia when she was showing a house, but the "antique collection" had been so unusual, she thought it sort of broke the ice.

Elvis, an antique? His cars, certainly. But Elvis? With those dreamy eyes and his polite Southern manners? Elvis, who cared so kindly for his mother, Gladys, who did the right thing and joined the Army and went to Germany, where he met the little girl who'd become his bride, with her tower of black hair and her eyes outlined like Gene Simmons's, a tiny baby in a pink blanket soon to appear in her arms?

"That Barbara Gillicut is really a battle-ax," my husband said. "Her husband cheats at golf, too. She's got those hippo hips and he's as thin as my putter. No wonder he's always sitting around the clubhouse drinking vodka tonics. I wouldn't want to be married to her." He put the screwdriver on the hall table. It always took him weeks to return anything to the basement after he'd made a repair or rehung a picture. And damned if I'd do it. Those things were his responsibility, as much as the kitchen was mine.

"Should I have taken it up with Ted when he said Elvis was gay?" he asked.

"Ted? Last night? He wasn't saying Elvis was gay. No one thinks Elvis was gay, even though old ladies loved him. Liberace was gay. Though I guess they've never even heard of Liberace, unless some of them watched that Michael Douglas movie. He was saying that the owner was gay. Jon Enders."

My husband considered the screwdriver. He scratched his earlobe. "Well, then, should I have said something about that, even if I misunderstood?"

"What would you have said?"

"I would have asked why he brought it up. Because stereotyping must have been underlying what he said. It was something of a non sequitur, I thought. Not that I was put here to offer guidance to the young."

He dialed Ted's number again. I knew that if Ted picked up, my husband was going to ask him who, exactly, he'd been calling gay. There's nothing my husband likes more than proving me wrong.

But the phone rang unanswered. And when my husband's phone finally bleated its "Yankee Doodle" ring (totally obnoxious, which, my husband said, was the point) and he answered, I was as surprised as he that it was not a guilty Ted, it was Barbara Gillicut, telling him he'd brought her luck. She'd gotten her first offer on the house. Her voice was almost girlish, he told me afterward—she sounded like a different person. She told him the story about the urn on the table before saying good-bye. "Oh god, is that cremains?" the prospective buyer said. Barbara was choking with laughter as she repeated this. No, she'd told the woman. It was the ashes of the owner's drawing pad. Her client had been trying for years to make a perfect drawing of a stone. It was the reason he'd bought the house, in what he always referred to as "the countryside." He had several stones he placed on the tabletop every day ("My god, he puts them to bed in a little satin drawstring pouch, like he's settling babies in their crib!"). He worked on his sketches night and day, and then when the pad was filled with his drawings, he . . . well, what did he do? Even Barbara Gillicut wasn't there when he must have done something. Had he showed all the deficient drawings to the Elvises? Poured himself a huge glass of cognac and drunk it down, weeping? But after that moment—I've come to believe life is defined in just such moments—he made the only fire he ever had in the fireplace. He'd told her explicitly; he'd said he hadn't lit a fire since Cub Scouts—and sent the sheets of paper up in flames. Only the spiral binder, singed, remained, and he said he was going to hang it on the chain that dangled from his porch fan—he'd kept his house outside of Boston, which turned out to be a good thing—and every time he turned on the fan, he'd remember what he called "the most humbling undertaking of my life."

In Barbara Gillicut's opinion, artists were right on the edge of insanity every moment. It seemed as if it must make some cosmic sense that she was the person from whom he'd bought his house, and she was the person he'd brought in to sell it, as well as the person to whom he told this story. Since she liked to remark on the obvious, she told me she was glad he hadn't burned the house down along with his drawings. He'd shoveled out the fireplace when the ashes were cold. He'd put them into his beautiful urn—an antique, handed down from his grandmother. (How many conversations had she had with him? We'd never seen her dropping by.) Then he'd listed the house with her, only a year or so after he bought it, and left with another man for Reykjavik ("Imagine! He didn't like these winters and he decamped for Iceland!") and now she was going to have the pleasure of giving him a huge thumbs-up across the miles, because she was very optimistic. She'd seen it in the spark of the woman's eyes that she wanted the house, and women's opinions prevailed.

My roommate during this time was an acting student named Eagle Soars. His English father had married an American who claimed her great-grandmother had Indian blood. Eagle Soars had been Eddie in school, but his birth certificate really did give his first and middle names as Eagle Soars (his last name, which he later dropped, was Stevens), and by the time he was twenty, he thought the name might be useful if he intended to act. He made extra money by giving Major Maybe his four p.m. walk down to Tenth Avenue, then up either Twenty-first or Twenty-second Street, down Eighth Avenue, then down Twentieth to home.

In those days, Chelsea was more of a mom-and-pop neighborhood. No art galleries, just a few sex clubs way west. There was a nice florist called Howe. I sometimes bought a single flower to take back to the apartment and make part of my little altar to the far left side of the deep windows that overlooked the backyard: a picture of my mother and father on their wedding day, in a little heart-shaped frame; my sister lying on a fur rug, looking dazed, the day they brought her back from the hospital; a badly faded snapshot of my first pet, Doris the cat; the deteriorating wrist corsage I'd worn to the senior prom, inside a Plexiglas box; one of my wisdom teeth dangling from a chain around the casement window handle. These things were grouped together in solidarity with Eagle Soars, whose own display featured a double photo frame showing both his high school graduation picture and a snapshot of the boy he had a crush on in high school, with a big bandage across his face after reconstructive surgery on his nose (bicycle accident); a pencil sharpener with a tutu-skirted hippopotamus in second position; a teaspoon stolen from the Plaza; the framed eviction notice from his previous landlord in Columbus, Ohio. It was a joke that when I had a new flower he'd move it to the right in the middle of the night, and when he was out walking the neighbor's dog, I'd put it back on my side. We split the weekly wine bill because neither of us drank more than the other. He was more interested in weed, and I was interested in not getting fat. Still, we went through a gallon a week of Italian white wine that the wine seller always said he wasn't going to have access to for long (but nothing would have made us spend our money on a whole case of wine).

The day of the incident with the dog and the red-haired lady, Soars and I were out on the little chairs that sat inside the iron fence in front of the brownstone, where a large pink hibiscus set out by the guy in the garden apartment added a huge amount of atmosphere. Also, he'd put circular cushions on the chairs, which made them so much easier to sit on. He was a psychologist whose specialty was adolescents. They'd arrive and depart with deep scowls, throwing down cigarettes and crushing them, rarely making eye contact with us. The psychologist had told us that it was better not to greet the clients because there was hardly anything you could say to them that would be correct. We accepted this and ignored their acne eruptions and fanned away their cigarette smoke and basically looked right through them unless they seemed so desperate to be friendly that we said the word "Hello." Once an ambulance came and got one of the clients from the basement who, we later found out (in spite of doctor-patient confidentiality) had been bleeding and had stuffed washcloths in his pants to come to his weekly appointment. The basement was called the "Garden Apartment." When the wisteria was in bloom, the psychologist took back his little chairs and added them to others in the yard behind the house and had a real champagne party, to which we were always invited. If he ever sat in the chairs when they were out front, we never once saw it. Then again, we were in them a lot, and he was a pleasant, polite man, so maybe he didn't have much of a chance.

We were doing acting exercises. Soars read his lines and at some point it was my job to interject something distracting, or to go into a fake coughing spasm, or even to say something hostile, such as "You miserable faggot, you're no Edward, let alone Lear!" The thought was, anything could happen during a performance and the actor had to squelch his real-life reaction and keep going, without faltering. There was only one script, since it cost money to Xerox, so we sat close together. I tried to act, myself, to the extent that I didn't want him to be able to anticipate one of my sneezes or outbursts, which I'd learned he could sense because of my breathing slightly altering in advance of speaking, or by my moving in even the smallest way, or by the minuscule noise my lips made when parting. My job was to zing him without warning. One time I actually threw myself off the chair and writhed like someone having a seizure. I'd deliberately worn long sleeves and jeans, so the damage was minor, but a delivery person wheeling seltzer cases into the brownstone next door stopped and ran to my assistance, and it was more than a little embarrassing when we had to explain.

I'm so sentimental. I can hardly believe there was such a time now. (I'm a doctor with a medical group in Portland, Maine; Soars is the divorced father of twins and an avid white-water rafter who leads trips for a tour company out west and writes articles about the outdoors and teaches at a community college.)

Here's an obvious thing that I never thought about until recently: Soars and I weren't just well suited to living together, we were so simpatico we morphed into an old married couple, in speeded-up time. For years, we were playacting the daily life of so many marriages, with my sudden, sometimes insane eruptions of temper, our long-standing joke about moving each other's tchotchkes, with his constantly repeated lines (though his, ideally, came from Shakespeare).

While he was still in New York, he decided that except for his big crush on one guy, he wasn't gay. He stopped dating men and began to hang out with me and my girlfriends, and then he began dating one of them, whose heart he broke, but that's another story; even if he's bi, time proved that he chose to marry women (he also had a second wife).

Anyway, as Soars and I were rehearsing that day, the red-haired lady stood up and cursed our dog friend, screaming, "Lucifer the devil! Luuuuuuucifer!" rushing poor, scared Major Maybe, who'd just lifted a leg to pee against his favorite tree in the tree box and was humiliated when he had to drop it midstream. She stretched out her arms and meant to topple Mr. Leavell, who simply turned sideways and let the wild tornado pass (Major Maybe, a peaceful fellow, had flattened himself on the ground), and so it did, twirling crazily from her little bare feet up her thick legs, her own long, pee-stained skirt tangling in a way that tripped her, so that when she continued her trajectory between parked cars, into Twentieth Street, howling that once the devil appeared there could be no redemption, the fabric was coiled around her like cotton candy. Then she was flung forward as if someone really had not enjoyed their treat. The cab screeched to a halt and the driver jumped out and bent over her like a referee giving the count, his finger scolding: woman down . . . until up she sprang, toppling a seminarian who, along with Mr. Leavell (who was in his sixties), rushed to pull her off the taxi driver, whom she was attempting to squeeze to death. Major Maybe was so humiliated that his jaw went flaccid, his leash having been tossed over one of the pointy spikes of the iron gate that enclosed the little cement area outside his home. The leash was too short for him to lie down without strangling, so he had to sit and watch the spectacle. He'd had an invigorating walk, lifted his leg for a few pees, and experienced some excellent sniffs—now this: an explosion from a street person sent our way by Fidel Castro, who'd released people from the mental hospitals and put them on ships and sent them here to mingle with our own. On good days she sang hymns in Spanish in a beautiful, clear soprano. She felt the breeze blow through her hair. She ate her saltines and did nothing to anyone. On bad days . . . well.

Where were the police? Where were the police? This was a time before cell phones. When the police arrived they handled the red-haired lady roughly, so much so that the seminarian took issue (it did no good). Her wrists were cuffed and her head was dunked into the police car like a basketball player sinking a one-handed shot. Easy. Nothing to it. Fast resumption of the game.

Our rehearsals were suspended. Mr. Leavell picked up his dog's leash and marched up the steps into his house.

Soars and I went upstairs and broke out the bottle of Italian white and sat in our director's chairs for a while—they were cheap, and the only furniture. Neither of us thought about stealing the flower to our side. Which was a rubrum lily that day, dropping its pollen onto the floor beneath the window, a giant's yellow dandruff. Outside, the wisteria vine was thick and green, curlicues and pointing witches' fingers of pale green shoots that would continue to quickly unfurl, but it was no longer in bloom. We took a walk. We discussed our futures. We wondered if we were going to fail, just simply fail: if I'd never know what I wanted to do in life (I worked part-time as a waitress and my mother sent a check every month that paid more than my half of the rent). We wondered if AIDS would sweep through the city, if the red-haired lady had enough sanity to be scared at the police station, how long Major Maybe would live. Soars reached for my hand. We never held hands because, of course, we weren't a couple. We laced our fingers, and I was astonished at how bony his hand felt, and that his palms were sweaty. Then we went back and fucked. We did what so many people do on someone else's wedding day, or after someone else's funeral, though in this case it was only on the day some street person got carted off to the police station. We had a good time doing it, but the only thing that changed was that for some reason, afterward, neither of us continued to play the game of Steal the Flower. I soon stopped buying them. I used the money to buy other little luxuries, like mascara. He continued dating my friend.

I met the man I married at a wedding I attended in Cape Neddick, Maine, in December (the bridesmaids carried white rabbit-fur muffs), though it took us eight years to get around all deception, right? You understand that the picture shows more space than exists. You fall for the vase of fresh flowers on the nightstand that in real life probably has the circumference of a pie pan. You know the neighborhood's hip without reading the specifics: Galleries! Bookstores! Chelsea Piers!

A whole vase of flowers in the photograph. So lavish, its extravagance conveying more than a sense of romance or the idea of a luxurious life inside a welcoming apartment. Flowers that will be picked up and whisked away after the shot, as the curtains are pulled together against the daylight that will fade the rug. Close down the set, bring on the travelers, light it up again.

Indelible, the yellow pollen on the floor.

ROAD MOVIE

Rose petals blew off the trellis, and the small pots of lantana outside each of the five motel rooms fell over in unison, like Lego pieces swiped by some kid's hand. Moira picked up a clump of dirt near her door and put it back in the pot, but she was on vacation, she didn't have to clean, she didn't want to ruin her manicure. She kicked aside a bit of what remained with the toe of her sneaker.

June in California was great, and the motel was amazing: the Nevada Sunset, in the Russian River Valley. She'd found it on the app that showed hotels discounted that day and managed to get the same rate for the rest of the week. It was Wednesday. She and Hughes wouldn't have to check out until Saturday at eleven. She knew at least one time when they'd be having sex: at ten forty-five Saturday morning. He loved to have sex before checking out of a motel. He just loved it.

Also (as he'd made clear) he loved his longtime girlfriend

who had never thrown him over, never had a problem with alcohol, didn't want children. This paragon, Elizabeth, was also conveniently allergic to pets and didn't eat red meat. Her negative traits were that she worked all the time and took calls from her colleagues up until midnight; she was borderline anorexic; she woke him up when she had nightmares about rabid animals; her mother, a psychiatrist, was always hovering. Most shocking of all, Elizabeth chewed cinnamon gum.

Moira herself had drawn up a list of pluses and minuses, half kidding, half hoping he'd see that he should break off his relationship with neurotic Elizabeth and make a commitment to her, instead. Drinking weak margaritas at the swimming pool wasn't helping her cause, though. (She was doing it because her impacted molar hurt. She didn't look forward to the surgery she was going to have in September to dig out this remaining molar. The other extraction had caused her a lot of problems and pain. Right now she was taking two or three more Advil Liqui-Gels at a time than the label suggested and trying not to think about fall.)

"It doesn't suggest. It tells you the correct daily dose," he'd said the night before, tossing the bottle of Advil aside, watching Louis C.K. on his iPad mini. She'd only been having a ginger ale at that point, from the vending machine at the end of the row of motel rooms. Like everyone, she'd brought *The Goldfinch* on vacation. He'd read two or three pages and not fought her over it. He was, at the moment, reading *The Economist* poolside.

Kunal, the nice young cleaning person with perfect posture, had been mobilized by the wind. He suddenly appeared with a broom, also pulling a wagon behind him carrying the ceramic planters he and the motel owner no doubt wished they'd gotten the plants into before the wind blew up. "More tonight, maybe no electricity, so there will later be flashlights, ma'am," Kunal said. "One time, no storm at all, squirrels did an acrobatic act on those power lines. See up there? No power for a day and a half. Some people came to play cards by the light of the oil lamp. I like the owner, who is very adaptable, as people often are in their second careers. He won at cards himself! He said, 'If I were Ben Affleck, and you were the casino owners, I'd be turned out of my own house!' Then later in the night he lost what he had won and some more. I've never seen him gamble before or after. Let me tell you, this job is so much better than driving a taxicab. Every morning he squeezes fresh orange juice for us. He says, 'Here's to whatever's going on in Silicon Valley,' and we clink rims." Kunal talked over his shoulder, going past all the doors, lowering the plants into the blue and green striped ceramic pots. "Okay, I think the Dustbuster is fine for this slight problem," he said to himself. Earphones were draped around his neck. He listened to what he called "native music" but was embarrassed if anyone asked to hear. "He's probably listening to porn tapes" had been Hughes's opinion, when it turned out both he and Moira had asked about what music was playing and Kunal had demurred both times. Usually you could hear a bit of sound leaking out, but neither had.

A storm. How dramatic. It would be another occasion to have sex. After sex, it might be another occasion to bring up their future, long term. Though to be honest, she wasn't one hundred percent sure she thought being with Hughes was a good idea. He was sort of a tyrant about personal cleanliness and watching one's weight and he even—this was unbelievable—wanted her to put on a hairnet when she prepared food. This, from someone who enjoyed the kind of sex he liked?

Five was an unusual number of motel units. Unit three, rented to a wan-faced Norwegian couple who could barely even pantomime English, was the largest, Kunal had told Hughes, when he asked. It had been formed from half of room number four, the rest of which had been converted into closet space. In the afternoon the closet door was often open and the owner's six-year-old daughter, of whom he had joint custody, could be seen doing her almost alarmingly good paintings of trees and the pool area across from the motel units, sitting at a little easel, listening to music through her own earbuds (She liked xx). She, Lark, had told them that her mother was "a burned-out hippie." She'd been surprised when they laughed. "What's funny?" she'd said, frowning. Hughes had quickly said something to spare her sensitive feelings. "We just don't remember that there were hippies, ourselves, most days, so that took us aback," he'd said. Why did he think he'd be such a bad father? He wouldn't. But she accepted that there was no way to change his mind.

She answered a call from her mother as she was undressing to take a shower, sweaty and itchy from the suntan lotion that felt like wet moss when it was applied. A white glob of wet moss. They were really going to have to buy a better brand. "Mom!" she said. "How goes?"

Her mother was at a spa, getting a pedicure. It was a lovely place, not one of those dubious Korean scrub joints, where the women looked off into space and chattered as they exfoliated your heels. Every now and then she and her mother made a day of it, ate lunch at the fabulous Thai restaurant, then had some wonderful treatment, followed by a neck massage. It had been a while, though. Her mother had been preoccupied with insurance problems Will had somehow caused by checking himself out of rehab midprogram and being gone for twenty-four hours before being readmitted. It was June, and her mother had not yet been able to pay their taxes, though she and Larry (her accountant) had filed for an extension.

"Are you at the Nevada Sunset motel, is that what you told me?" her mother asked.

"Yeah. About to step into the shower. And I'm not just making that up. Why?" she said.

"Because today I heard about two places—I wrote both of the names down, because one sounded so familiar. Have you heard of Hope's Cottages, in Healdsburg?"

"No. Why?"

"Well, Larry's wife came with me to the spa, and their son is interning for some protégé of Roman Polanski's, and that young man is going to be doing a film at two places, and one of them is the motel you're staying at, and the other one is the cottages place. I forget—some famous musician lives in Healdsburg, who's doing the sound track. You'd know the name if I could remember it."

"When's this happening? You think they might need extras?"

"Oh, I remember when you did want to be an actress, and then when you sang and played guitar with your brother and you two harmonized with those sweet voices, and his singing was almost as high as yours. He became a tenor, which amazes me. He loves to sing again, did I tell you that? They've formed a band with some sarcastic name. Last week he called in the middle of the afternoon to apologize to me for all the trouble he'd caused. I know they make them do that."

"They can't make them."

"Then they said they'd double their meds and give them no ice cream, or something. I don't know. It's not that pleasant to get calls like that in the middle of the afternoon. I was having a quiet moment, and suddenly there was your brother's voice, all choked up. He went into the whole thing about the skirmish last year when he got back to my car and it had been booted. I had to live through that again, his punching the policeman. What a traumatic day."

"I love you and I'm happy to hear from you, but I'm naked and greasy with suntan lotion, so can I call back?"

"Don't bother. But you do know there's a storm coming? Maybe they'll be checking in to make a horror movie, or one of those vampire things that I'm not supposed to call 'horror movies.' Larry's daughter has written a script for one of those at UCLA. He wanted me to read it, as though I could differentiate one from another. You're not going to do anything stupid, like break up Hughes's relationship with Elizabeth, are you? It kills me that I have to know you're at a motel with a friend's daughter's boyfriend."

"Anorexic bitch," Moira said.

"I'm not going to respond to that," her mother said. "You

remember that if Hughes cheats on her with you, he'll cheat on you with someone else. But I really only called to say I love you no matter what you do and because of the strange coincidence of the Polanski thing. Well, it's a small world. Not that he can move around it freely. Anyway, Daddy sends love. He's doing great today. He loves the new afternoon attendant. They go to a park and listen to birdcalls together. Your father has two pairs of binoculars that would allow anyone living here to see into Buckingham Palace. Love you. Bye."

"Bye," she said.

There was a knock on the door. Hughes had, as usual, forgotten his key? (Real keys! So cool.) She wrapped the towel around her and said, "Yes?" at the door.

"I have free drink coupons for a new bar that opened a few nights ago. We would like you to have them," Kunal said.

"Thank you, Kunal. Can you just push them under the door? No. I guess you can't. Can I get them from you when I get out of the shower? I was just—"

"Extremely sorry," Kunal said. "Hughes said to please give them to you. He said he loses everything."

She opened the door a crack and reached out. Two pieces of paper were put in her hand. "Thanks so much," she said, to Kunal's embarrassed, trailed off "Sorry to interrupt."

In the distance she could hear the wind rustling the trees. It was great they didn't need air-conditioning. She heard faint music she knew was not Kunal's, so maybe it was wind chimes. The towel was nice, thick enough, neither limp nor stiff. She'd brought her own favorite soap with her. Kunal had liked it so much, she'd given him the other bar (lemon verbena and sage). Every day, they left a note for Kunal saying simply, "Thank you," and a ten-dollar bill. They'd found a vase of ivy near the book on the night table, with one white daisy plunked in the center of the real glass vase. Now, there were free drink coupons.

She stepped into the shower. Her mother was right about Hughes cheating. But what if they had a few good years? Or what if the cheating was somehow, miraculously, kept secret? What if she cheated? That wouldn't be impossible, would it? As she began to smell like an herb garden, she thought: Elizabeth, with your smell of roses, just find someone else. You'd never lighten up enough to have a drink at a bar, even if it was free, would you? You could just disappear, Elizabeth, like a strand of hair going down the drain. After every shower, she herself had to dab up any hair that might have fallen with a crumpled Kleenex. It was gross, but Hughes thought finding hair in the drain was grosser. When she turned the water off, she realized she'd forgotten to wind the towel around her hair and it was damp. How preoccupied with that woman am I? she wondered. Then she stepped out onto the bath rug that even Hughes agreed was totally clean and began to towel off, first blotting her stomach, then gathering the towel together to rub it over her pubic hair. She had the legs of a young girl, athletic and unmarred. She'd inherited them from her mother, though her mother had also been responsible for her not very pretty mouth. She resisted looking in the mirror.

"Hughes!" she called, as she walked across the parking lot toward the pool. He was underwater, clutching his knees. Bubbles rose to the surface. Yes, there were wind chimes on the lower branch of the tree at the far side of the pool. She hadn't noticed them before.

"What a beauty!" he said when he surfaced, shaking his head; tilting it, really, to get water out of his ears. "How do I deserve such a beautiful woman and free drink tickets besides?"

"I thought you didn't approve of my drinking."

"Free?" he said.

They laughed. They laughed when they watched Jon Stewart, often. When they watched old *Fawlty Towers*. He thought Louis C.K. was a riot. She laughed, a little meanly, when he reached into food she'd prepared in her apartment and brought out an infinitesimally thin strand not of hair but the stem of some herb, a bit of oregano, something like that. On a scale of one to one hundred, she thought she loved him more than eighty.

"It's not going to storm. It blew over," he said, climbing one-handed up the ladder. "This situation with Bezos and the *Washington Post* is an interesting one. He wasn't so high and mighty he didn't get in touch with Bob Woodward right away for advice. He—Bezos, I mean—has got a skunk works team in New York now, called WPNYC, which is a great idea. I think he's going to turn it around."

"Skunk works?" she said. The wind chimes were tinkling in the breeze. She was not so sure the storm had passed over.

"How about a little fooling around, followed by a brief nap, then drinks?" he said.

"How much do you love me, on a scale of one to one hundred?" she said.

Oh god, whatever had made her ask that? What, what, what.

He tucked in his chin. Water streamed down his body, which was a good body. He worked out. His business partner had turned out to be a genius, but an out-of-shape one, so Hughes had become the front man. One of Hughes's first moves had been to hire his old school buddy from Maine, who was a dynamite deal finalizer, though lately he'd been complaining about all the commuting from Maine to California.

Moira, looking at Hughes, thought: Would he have said exactly the same thing to Elizabeth, would he have called her beautiful, if he'd brought her to the Nevada Sunset?

"One hundred," he said, after too much delay. "But if we could please put relationship talk on hold? I'm not in the mood today, Moira, I'm really not."

To change the subject, she said, "My mother called. She sends you her best. She said that of all things, she found out some movie is going to be filmed at this motel. Not today, I wouldn't guess. Except for the Norwegians, nobody seems to be checking in regardless of the price, which is odd."

"You don't think this place is just a bit obscure?"

"Not really. An app directed us here." She shrugged. If he said one hundred, she thought he, too, might love her about as much as she loved him: eighty. Eighty, max.

"How's your brother?" he asked halfheartedly. He liked her brother more than he let on. They'd done some major hikes together in the White Mountains, and he'd treated her brother to a week in Hawaii, when he and the Genius had gone there to talk to clients. They'd flown in a helicopter over a waterfall.

"I don't know. She didn't really say anything about him. But Daddy has a new attendant he likes. That's good news. He mostly hates people."

"Getting out?"

"Yes. He went to the park today. Or maybe it was yesterday. I don't remember."

"We should take him somewhere in the van again."

"Well, we're not a couple, so we can't very easily do that, since Elizabeth's parents live two doors down from my parents."

He squinted at her. Seventy, max. Whenever he was being truly selfless, she went in for the kill. That was what he'd said about her at the beginning of the last trip, and she hadn't forgotten it. He'd made her sound like a dangerous fish.

Thunder, but no lightning.

"I'm not in the mood anymore. I think I'll get with your program. Where are those coupons?" he said.

"On the table by the door."

"Are you going to snap out of it, or should I look forward to an evening of sulking?" he said.

"Do you think you might be picking a fight?" she said. "A few minutes ago you loved me one hundred percent, and I was a beautiful woman."

"But what are you doing with your life? I mean, really. You toss off that editing in your sleep, almost. You were going to start a book, weren't you? How many people really have the talent to write a good book, but you do."

"Oh, go drinking with Bob Woodward," she said, standing up and walking away.

"I've only met him once," Hughes said. "I'm afraid I don't have his contact information. I don't think he'd be interested in flying out here and meeting me at the Nevada . . ."

She went into the room and put the chain on the door. He'd be too embarrassed to let anyone see she'd shut him out. Well, that was what she got for telling Hughes her dream. She was glad she hadn't shown him the first fifty pages of the manuscript, as she'd been tempted to, when Elizabeth had been given a raise at work. She'd gotten yet another raise— the second in less than a year—and she and her stupid sister were now on a trip to Provence, a girls' road trip to Aix, Avignon, and Arles. The three As, and wasn't that just perfect? Such A-plus girls, both of them, one a scarecrow with minor Madonna pecs and hair that fell out because of a nutritional deficiency, the other fat.

The door jerked and trembled. "Oh, this is just so childish," he said. "What would you do if I got in the car and drove away, huh?"

She considered this and grudgingly opened the door. "Show some respect," she said, keeping her voice even. "This is not easy for me, and may I remind you, I am not in control of the situation."

"I'm sorry. I'll take a quick shower and we can get out of here," he said.

"I've never seen you quite so excited about a free drink," she said.

"I always go to hotel lobbies if they have free wine, don't I?"

"That's different."

"It's not much different," he said. "I loved that place in Philadelphia: the Hotel Monaco."

"You sent me a selfie of yourself there," she said. "I remember the name. It reminded me of Grace Kelly. Were she and what's his name, Cary Grant, lovers or just friends?"

"Don't know," he said, going into the bathroom.

She stretched out on the bed. She noticed that today there were three daisies amid the ivy. On the notepad by the bed was written, "You are welcome." She smiled, then instantly worried that for some reason, Hughes might not like to know their note had been answered. He always tried to seem like a nice guy by telling everyone to call him by his first name, but had his limits with people. She really liked Kunal, wished he could be her father's attendant—Kunal, her father would be sure to like—but Hughes drew lines in the sand about people: yes, the haircutter was nice, but she was just a haircutter. That sort of thing. She crumpled the note and stuffed it in her pocket. "I do love you, I do, Hughes," she whispered. She'd made no further progress with the thick novel on the night table. She listened to the water in the shower. She wondered if the owner's daughter would be painting in the little storage room in the afternoon. She so appreciated her own parents staying together. It hadn't saved her brother, but then, whatever problems he had probably had little to do with them. They'd been good parents. Pretty good. Her father hadn't, as the expression went, been very present. Neither, together or separately, could ever have been one of the demons he'd tried to chase away with cocaine and shots. Shots. She certainly no longer did shots. That was gone, like dancing all night until sunup.

*   *   *

When they returned after having two free drinks apiece (their choice! They'd tried G and Ts with that new gin, Tanqueray Ten), then ordering veggie burgers and leaving a sizable tip, there was some action at the motel. Rooms glowed at each end like luminous bookends. The Norwegians were in their room, but the curtains were closed, so the light was not very noticeable. Only one room remained empty, and Moira felt vaguely happy for the motel owner but also a little disappointed, since so far they'd had such a private vacation. Which was also one day closer to ending. Which increased the pressure to have the talk—to at least give it one more try; to see if they could arrive at any conclusion, even temporary, that might make her feel better, that might be an incentive to get back to work. He was correct that editing the scientific pieces only took a few hours a week now, since the Internet was so much help and she was working with such professional writers that they sent almost all the primary source material to her along with their pieces. The things she'd found out about moth communication. The amygdala. A rare orchid that bloomed underground whose stems might be useful in pain management. Fracking (so depressing).

Two SUVs were wedged into one and a half parking spaces. A motorcycle sat at the opposite end. The motel owner was standing outside the office, chatting with someone inside. She and Hughes waved as they opened their door. Hughes immediately turned on the TV. She went to the bathroom. She peed and fingered her arm for the little matchstick-size Nexplanon the doctor had injected near her armpit. What the doctor had said was true: you could locate it with no trouble, but you couldn't see it. No birth control pills for her; she'd read enough about what harm they did after a certain age (she was three years older than he). She brushed her hair and thought to put the loose strands into a Kleenex and drop it in the trash basket. Yet again, she avoided looking in the mirror as she took the clip out of her hair and let it fall to her shoulders. Past her shoulders, and her mother didn't approve. "It makes you look older, not younger!" she always said. Her eyes flicked to the mirror, then down. She didn't have much of a sense of how old she looked. Men still tried to pick her up sometimes. Hughes had called her beautiful. So next would come sex with Hughes, a Coke or a ginger ale from the machine, maybe a little package of Hydrox to split, if he was in a really good mood. There was a knock at the door and she waited while Hughes answered it.

"The people who have just checked in are from Hollywood. Good evening, Hughes. I'm sorry I am so excited, I have hurried to state this information, but the two men in unit one have me a little upset, due to the urgency of their request. They need to light the parking lot and wonder if you will be inconvenienced by their doing that. We did not know about this until only one hour ago, perhaps less. I phoned your room, but you were not back yet. We understand totally if this would not be what you want."

"What do you mean, Kunal? They're making the motel into a movie set?"

"Yes, that is exactly it, but they are not now making a

movie. They will send a video to the director, and he must decide how to proceed. To be honest, this is a sudden plan and yes, we will be given some money, though we honor the wishes of our other guests, and except for perhaps buying you dinner—if you have not had dinner—we are wondering whether the matter of a couple of hours would truly inconvenience you."

"It's fine," Moira said, coming out of the bathroom. Her molar hurt, as well as the place she'd rubbed repeatedly under her arm. "No big deal. Can we watch?"

Hughes turned toward her. She could see that he was about to say something, then decided against it. She had a quick flash of them the night before—no, two nights before—entangled on the bed, the sweat on his face, the curtains not pulled together tightly enough, but no one was there, no one but the Norwegians, who seemed to sleep all day and night.

"Of course," Hughes said. "But yes, do ask if we keep out of their way, whether we could sit back by the pool and watch."

"I will ask," Kunal said. "Thank you. Tomorrow night, Mr. Reed would like to buy you dinner, then. You have been a pleasure to have at the motel."

"You sound like you're out of central casting," Hughes said, smiling a bit.

"Sir?"

Again, Hughes altered his expression. "I mean, we all suddenly become extras, or something," he said. "We'll just sit out by the pool and see if this amuses us."

"Okay," Kunal said, bowing slightly as he turned away.

Then he stopped and turned toward the still-open doorway. "I turn like that man, Columbo!" he said. "Do you remember that show? He would take his leave and then turn and say, 'One more thing,' or something like that?"

"Yes," Hughes said, smiling. "Peter Falk. That was a great show."

"So for this minute I become Columbo," Kunal said. "Were you saying before—this is my one more thing—did you mean I said something that sounded like an actor who would be hired from central casting?"

"What?" Hughes said. "I was just joking."

"Of course. It's what I thought," Kunal said, turning without bowing. "Good, then, I will make arrangements for you to sit outside."

Hughes shook his head and closed the door. He'd lied. He'd suddenly realized Kunal was a stereotype. A stock character.

"People do notice when you're being a shit. You must realize that. I happen not to be able to do without you, but you're far from a perfect person."

"That's a backhanded compliment," he said.

"No, it's a straightforward comment. I save my backhand for tennis."

"Well, aren't you the clever person?"

"Let's leave that a rhetorical question and not miss the goings-on."

"Really?" he said suddenly. "You'd get off on watching some stupid movie made in this obscure little motel? That's your best thought for tonight?"

"You could have said no," Moira said, sliding her hands

in the pockets of her Bermuda shorts. "Were you deferring to me when you agreed it would be great to have everything lit up? Or maybe you were deferring to the servant, Kunal?"

"The servant? He's not my servant. What the fuck! You're this way on two drinks?"

"That's a low blow. You know two drinks certainly are not affecting anything I say."

"Oh, okay, I'll just throw open the door and they can film around us. They can get two for the price of one: some pointless couple arguing in their little room and then whatever else they're filming."

"Listen to yourself. You think you're pointless?"

"You can be so maddening, Moira. You listen, yourself. You're being a bitch. Let's not do this, okay? Let's sit outside."

"Sure, sure, the world's for our entertainment," Moira said, walking past him.

The wind chimes tinkled. Would the film people take them down? Or would they like ambient sound? In the distance, the owner raised a hand again as he hurried into the locked closet and came out with a vacuum, which he carried to the man with the motorcycle in the far room. There were five or six—six—men already in the parking lot. "Don't move the cars, leave 'em where they are," one shouted. "No way!" another shouted back. "We move the cars and see what the light's like first." "That's unnecessary, I'm telling ya," the first man said. Well—good. They wouldn't have to move their car.

In front of the fence around the pool sat two chairs side by side. Moira sat in one, unnoticed by the work crew. Hughes came out of the motel room, pulling the door shut. She could only hope he'd remembered a key, since she hadn't. Not like her, but she'd been rattled.

She saw the key flash in his hand, then his hand plunge into his pants pocket. Or she saw no such thing—she saw only that something was being held, something disappeared. "Have the key?" she said, trying to sound casual.

"Yup," he said. He sat down beside her. He said, "I'm surprised he didn't put a table between the chairs and maybe drag out two of those plastic footstools."

She looked at him. He looked older than she expected in the shadows. "Maybe free popcorn's still to come," she said, again trying to sound neutral. Casual and neutral: were they the same thing? Was she going to be wondering about little distinctions when she was old and gray—was she going to be one of those stereotypes, the amoral woman who does whatever she wants, but who never gets what she wants, because she doesn't even know what that would be?

Out of the corner of her eye she saw the Norwegian couple, the woman in a cropped top and tight silver pants, the man in jeans and pointed-toe boots and a Western shirt in a crazy shade of yellow decorated with dark brown arrows. The Norwegians? Was this their version of going native? "Over there, step out of that light into that other one," the older man called and they moved immediately, in unison, where they were told to go. The woman's hair looked longer than Moira remembered. Maybe it was extensions. They were clearly actors. Part of the film. Startled at the same realization, Hughes punched her lightly in the arm. "The ghouls are stars!" he said. "What do you know!"

Kunal came out of the Norwegians' room, carrying an ice

bucket holding an upended bottle. He didn't look in their direction. "Move more to the left, that's right," one of the men rolling lights said to the couple. "You know what you're doing, right?" They nodded. Hughes continued to stare, slowly shaking his head. Kunal and the owner stood outside the office in a huddle. "James, back it up a little," one of the men called to another. "That's right, follow Rick. I think I fucked up placing that last camera over there."

The Norwegians stood shoulder to shoulder. Tinkle, tinkle went the wind chimes. Twinkle, twinkle, little star, Moira thought. How I wonder what you are. She'd once played that, slowly, on her xylophone. Her brother had taught her how to read music. Her father had taught her to play tennis, then beat her every time. Her mother had taught her that kindness was a virtue and tried to see that her two children lived that way, even if her husband started fights in restaurants and once deliberately knocked over a glass of water on a tablecloth.

She was on her feet before she realized she was in motion. It was now thought that actions often started first, and explanations or rationalizations followed: I jumped up because I was mad! No, the person jumped up and then had to find a reason why.

Moira said to Kunal, "I know you're busy, but I wanted to apologize for him. We're not married, you know, and he's never going to marry me, but that's neither here nor there. You've seen to it that we had a lovely time here, and he appreciates that as much as I do. He's just one of those guys. You read him right. I apologize." She leaned forward slightly, the owner looking at her, perplexed. She kissed Kunal lightly on his forehead, a chaste, sister-brother kiss, which startled him and made him blush, though she could see from the sparkle in his eye that it was okay.

"Thank you," he said quietly. He turned to the motel owner, who held the ice bucket out to him. With his thumb in the slushy, cold water, Kunal took a step backward. He said to the owner, "What does it mean, 'neither here nor there'?"

THE LITTLE
HUTCHINSONS

On their way to their summer house, the Little Hutchinsons stopped in to say hello to us every summer. If you're curious about why they were called the Little Hutchinsons, it's because Al Hutchinson was six foot three—a basketball player, later a coach, from North Carolina—who married a very short woman from Bangor, Maine, and together they produced three sons, the tallest about five foot seven. The other boys, including our friend Gilly (the youngest), were about my height, which is five foot two.

I'm not obsessed with height, but it's the obvious thing to ask about someone called "little." The Senior Hutchinsons died when their private plane went down. Neither of the older boys wanted their house, uninsulated and in need of repair, though beautifully situated above cliffs that staggered like the nude descending a staircase down to a small, pebbly beach.

Etta Rae, who had not particularly enjoyed visiting her husband, Gilly's, parents when they were alive because of the amount of work it required helping them plant and prune flowers and bushes, making the meals, washing up . . . Etta Rae totally changed her impression of the house and of life in Maine after the tragedy that befell the Senior Hutchinsons. Every summer since, they've vacationed during June and July in the house, renting it out in August.

My husband and I live in the town you have to drive through to get to the big houses on the cliff above the beach. Our house is near the stone bungalow that used to be the library. I was quite surprised when Etta Rae asked if Marcy, their only child, might have her wedding party in our backyard. The house they inherited is a big, beautiful Victorian. There's even a cupola at the edge of the property, though it's lacking most of its roof. Etta Rae told me that they'd been advised that because of the direction the wind usually blew when there was a storm, a tent pitched in their backyard would be inadvisable in the event of bad weather on Marcy and Jasper's wedding day. Marcy was marrying her third cousin, who had cut our lawn every summer when he was going to Colby. They'd met in college, having seen each other only once during their childhoods. He'd been a problem child who'd been sent away to boarding school in Baltimore when he was younger, but he'd returned to Maine for college.

Marcy was a petite girl who wore heels or platform shoes or boots with stacked heels, no matter the fashion. Her husband-to-be was even shorter. For a man, he was quite short. When Marcy and her fiancé were out walking, people sometimes collided with them because they didn't see them coming—especially when one or the other was disembarking from a parked car. I liked Marcy, but I was less sure about

Jasper, though years had passed since he'd last been called before a judge. He'd gone to drug rehab and gotten clean. Still, there was something about him I didn't trust. I expected him to erupt someday, or to cause trouble eventually—what kind, I couldn't have anticipated. This fear figures in the story because, as crazy as I thought the request was to use our backyard to erect a tent when they lived on beautiful property overlooking a beach, I might simply have said yes if not for the fact that I once saw Jasper deliberately run the lawn mower over a turtle. He wasn't a child when he did this; he was a junior at Colby.

Etta Rae did not make her request in my husband's presence. We had our annual lunch of lobster rolls and herbal iced tea at the hotel across the road from the newish park full of rugosa roses and, in recent years, an assortment of tall grasses. As we sipped our tea, she told me that anxiety about the wedding was raising her blood pressure and that her husband, Gilly, was quite upset about it. He had even, behind her back, offered to give a considerable sum of money to the young couple if they would elope. Apparently at least the groom had considered this a good idea, but their daughter very much wanted a celebration. Could they elope and would her parents still give them a party, a bit after the fact, in June or July? They would. But because two companies who erected tents had expressed doubt about the safety and security of structures pitched above the cliffs (the gazebo would hold about six people and would have been useless, even if in perfect condition), Gilly had the idea—at least according to Etta Rae—that they ask if we'd be willing, as an alternative, to have the party at our house.

I said all the expected things: How would the bridal couple feel about that? Wouldn't they want to have the celebration inside their parents' house if the weather was bad? It seemed that the answer was complicated by the problem of Etta Rae's blood pressure. There were so many antiques, and she didn't know what she would do with them. She knew that I knew how disrespectful young people were now. They'd put out a cigarette, which they'd had the nerve to light up on the step right outside the kitchen door, in a Limoges dish. One of her daughter's friends had picked up a bisque figurine of a beckoning mermaid and used it as a back scratcher! Etta Rae always made me laugh. It makes me sound superficial, but I don't like to hear other people's problems, though I'll tolerate most anything if they take me aback and make me laugh. Etta Rae was the perfect storm in that way.

I tried to change the subject, but she was having none of it. She'd already lost ten pounds, and the blood pressure had not come down. She was determined to lose more weight. She'd just bought a book called *Wheat Belly* and was surprised I hadn't heard of it. She was not going to cleanse, however. (As she was elaborating on her opposition to cleansing, the waitress approached with the pitcher of iced tea, but quickly turned away before refilling our glasses.) By the time more iced tea was poured, Etta Rae had sweetened the deal (and I'm not talking sugar packet dumped in tea): she and Gilly would like to express their appreciation by giving me a day at the spa and buying Jamie an expensive putter they knew he coveted. People would tend our yard before and after the ceremony. All we had to do was say yes, save Etta Rae's life, and enjoy the party along with fifty or so other people. I said that I'd speak to Jamie. She clasped my hand. "This is not blush on my cheeks," she said, hovering her fingers.

As you might expect of someone who'd make this request of a friend, she'd had many ideas I thought were odd over the years. One had been to buy an empty building in Asheville, North Carolina, and to convert it to an old-age home for five couples (we could be the first to choose our floor). She sent me photographs of the building and floor plans in a mailing tube. Another time, she asked us to invest in a business that would involve protecting the reef off Key West by hiring people in shark costumes to scare people snorkeling or scuba diving, because their flippers inadvertently caused damage to the reef. She always had some crazy idea. While I found many of them amusing (not so the dreadful building she'd found in North Carolina, with fire damage and the roof caved in), I was perturbed by her most recent request.

"Let's say no," I said to my husband. "Why should someone have a wedding reception in our backyard, where years ago they deliberately killed a poor defenseless turtle?"

"He's turned into a nice young man," my husband said. "I once threw a dead raccoon down a well because I hated the people who ran the summer camp."

"She acts like some sitcom character, always spewing complications. I don't want a smelly Porta Potti in our backyard and people trampling the flowers."

"Then call her and tell her that."

"I'd sound like some neurotic, uncharitable woman who needed to lighten up."

"Well, isn't that the case?"

"Every time I tell you a problem that involves something

Etta Rae wants, you take it as an excuse to let me know I have deficiencies," I said. "She provokes fights in our marriage."

"Call her and tell her that."

"Why don't you call Gilly, man-to-man, and say we don't want to volunteer our backyard."

He lowered the newspaper. "Tell me exactly why we can't do it," he said. "Portable toilets?"

"She probably thinks the guests should go inside the house!" I said.

"We do have two and a half bathrooms. Certainly some guests would want to do something that day other than pee."

"What about my own antiques?"

"You're a big girl," he said. "If you don't want to do this, be honest about it. She'll understand. She'll have to. Or they won't be our friends anymore, if that's the way it turns out." He shrugged. On the front page of the *New York Times*, Obama's sideways expression was one of intense sorrow.

"That's part of the problem," I said. "I'm a big girl. They're so self-conscious about their height. It seems like we're lording it over them that we're big and powerful and can make any decision we want."

"Well, we can, about our house."

"She'll give me that look," I said. "Like a crab who's just had one claw ripped off so somebody can eat it, who knows before it's tossed back in the water that it's going to have to regenerate."

"I appreciate the analogy, but ask yourself: do I sound rational?"

I didn't, but neither was Etta Rae. Her house was far superior to ours. Why should we go along with her rather audacious request? But I did hate to disappoint her, and the truth was she had to go through life wobbling everywhere in her high heels and dealing with her husband's insecurity because he'd been so picked on during his childhood. For years, before they married, Gilly had seen a psychologist in Chelsea about his feelings of inferiority. One night, fishing around in his martini, standing with the three of us on our front porch, he'd scrutinized the dripping green olive and said, "If they'd invented bowling with midgets back then, I'd have been a human bowling ball."

Zelda-land. That had been her proposed name for our old people's apartment building. Zelda-land.

The next day I called and told her no. I apologized for being so uptight. I invoked my inherited collection of Steuben glass birds and mentioned the many expensive art books on the floor-to-ceiling shelves. I exaggerated the problem with our toilets barely flushing. I said I had to entertain my great-aunt, and I wasn't sure when she and her companion would be visiting (true). As she listened silently, I added a few more qualms, then invited them to dinner. She said, "I am so surprised and disappointed, I cannot think what to say."

They did come to dinner, but it was awkward. She didn't call again all summer, though somehow her husband sent a signal, and he and Jamie had a couple of games of golf. Then came the end of July. The situation had ruined my summer. We didn't know when the party was given, and we certainly weren't invited. We found out about it from the FedEx man, who'd been hired to play music with his band. I will always feel as guilty as I imagine an older, wiser boy would feel for having lawn-mowered a turtle in his youth.

The weather that day was everyone's worst scenario. It was overcast, then fiercely sunny, then gray clouds accumulated and raced forward like cars escaping rush-hour gridlock. Then began a pounding rain. They'd found a tent company earlier in the week that had come from Boston—cocky guys who said that barring a tsunami, their tent would hold. It didn't, and the groom was leaning against a pole when the entire thing lifted up like an enormous parachute that carried him out over the beach, where rain pounded down like arrows in the *Iliad*. He went up, up, then down. His hands must have lost their grip on the cloth. While the few drunks who didn't know what was happening partied on, he was launched like a sailor wrapped in a broken topsail, then fell from a great height onto the rocky beach, where he lay unconscious with a broken pelvis, broken arm, and three snapped ribs.

When I heard this, it made me remember a guide my husband and I had once hired, who'd told us, at the Cliffs of Moher, that the updraft was so fierce that if you threw someone over the edge, they might blow right up again—except in this case the groom didn't reappear. By the time we found out, the FedEx guy had written a song about it, but as he said to me, "It's no 'Sad-Eyed Lady of the Lowlands.'"

It will be on my conscience forever, of course: the revenge of the universe for the groom's mercilessness toward a fellow creature. But in what way does the dainty little doll-bride deserve such a thing, to have the dripping fist of fate grab her tiny companion and hurl him to earth in splinters? In the great flip-book of heaven, where our movement is created and the story reveals itself, what's to be made of some tragedy in miniature: not two people embracing to waltz with perfect steps and swirling tux tails and a voluminous skirt; not an agile fox chasing a rabbit that outwits him at the last second by burrowing into the hole of a tree . . . instead, one tiny figure approaching another, clasping that person's hand, both turning to face the viewer and to take a modest bow, then suddenly we see only the legs of one figure who levitates, the toes of tiny shoes dangling atop the page. Then nothing. Only the bride. White space.

Our flipping thumb runs out of space and time. We can only raise our first finger in the universal sign: a lesson must be learned.

Having learned it, I pass it on.

THE STROKE

"We don't like the children."

"We do love them, though."

"Doesn't matter. We want them to go away."

"I don't want Amity to go. She came all the way from Santa Cruz. And I'm sure she didn't really want to come."

"She criticized your new glass frames. Then she bragged about her vacation. We don't like to hear about other people's vacations."

"The worst thing is that she's still with that Andrew. How can she stand that braying voice? At least we didn't have to hear about Turks and Caicos from him, talking through that big nose like it's a megaphone."

"Remember when the hurricane was coming and the police cars came around with recordings blasting, telling us to leave the island?"

"We were dancing inside Harry Burns's new house. We just kept dancing. He had those expensive shutters that rolled down and locked, so we were inside with the lights on until they all went out."

"Key West was such a disaster. It would have gotten more attention if New Orleans hadn't been destroyed."

"And our little Kenneth, living in the Garden District. He thinks we care that he's gay, and we don't care. We've run out of different ways to insist that we're happy if he's happy. He glowered even as a little child. Maybe his bad eyes are hereditary."

"You should talk. Wouldn't you know that your pigeon-toed walk would be exactly the way poor Amity perambulates. None of the other goslings ever walked that way. She imitated everything you did. She still holds her hand out like it's got a cigarette in it, and you gave up smoking thirty years ago."

"Don't you like the way they all chipped in for presents? For, excuse me, modern things? You can bet Kenneth bullied them all into that."

"I don't want any of those things. I like to make tea with loose tea in a tea ball. I hate tea bags, and I certainly don't need a machine to make tea."

"It's modern."

"That did make him sound so gay, didn't it? 'You need some new things, some modern things.' Jesus."

"Do you think they're trying to hear us? I always thought they were listening like little foxes when we were fucking. Now I guess they know we're not doing that."

"We could listen intently and see if any of them are masturbating."

"No one does that in their parents' house. They forget they have genitals."

"And didn't you think Henry went on a little too long about the failure of the human pyramid? No one wants people to fall at a circus, but that's old news. I think he just didn't know what to talk about."

"He never got over not being accepted at your alma mater."

"Most people would think Stanford was every bit as impressive as Yale."

"Well, but he's not as rich as his classmates. He's still brooding about not making it off the wait list at Yale."

"He and Kenneth don't seem very buddy-buddy, the way they did when they were younger. Into their twenties, I mean. After that it seems Kenneth only wanted to talk about how the gay world operates, which I notice he's finally shut up about."

"They all get along. I was happy to hear that Amity thought she and Jason might visit Kenneth in Brooklyn."

"He's got a place big enough to hold the next circus."

"I know. I still don't understand how he could afford it, even with those two Russian girls living in the basement."

"Garden apartment."

"I don't like euphemisms."

"You have divinely dimpled thighs."

"I have a major cellulite problem."

"Let's make noise so they think we're fucking."

"They wouldn't think that. They'd think you were trying to strangle me, or something."

"Speaking of which, I think it's absolutely ridiculous that you've got a scarf coiled around your throat even when you're in your nightgown. As if I care about the tightness of the skin on your neck."

"You wear lifts in your shoes."

ANN BEATTIE

"I don't. They're orthotic inserts."

"We love to bitch at each other, don't we. Remember when we had real arguments? I hated your secretary. I still resent how bossy she was. Or I resent how cowardly you were in her presence. It bothered you so much that she was overqualified for the job. Why didn't you hire someone unqualified?"

"Say that again. I like to see your expression when you say 'unqualified.' Also, may I ask why you're suddenly sitting on the bed staring at me and acting like I'm obliged to be the evening's entertainment?"

"Well, you're a helluva lot better than having to sit out there with them watching *Breaking Bad* shows they missed. Though Amity isn't. She's knitting and trying to be sociable. I taught her some things too well."

"I taught Kenneth to fish and he lost the fishing pole. And Amity crashed the car in driver's ed. Remember that?"

"Don't bring it up to her anymore, even if you do find it so funny. I'm serious about that."

"Can't you say 'unqualified' again?"

"Why don't you have your pajamas on?"

"Because I've suddenly become very old and terribly tired. If I didn't have a machine to brew my tea, I might never have the mental energy to make tea again. Let alone climb onto a riding mower. I'm senile, and I'm afraid of that big new shiny machine. It'd be like jumping onto the back of a bull."

"Put your pajamas on."

"I don't think I'll wear them anymore. I think I'll skinny dip into bed."

"I don't care what you do, but I'm about to turn off the light."

158

"We haven't had our ritual!"

"That's out. We've got to live in the modern world. We have to change our old habits. I see that now. I don't care if you skip it tonight, but please do something other than mock the children's good intentions."

"You like the tea machine?"

"I do not. But I'm not fixated on it."

"It will have to be visible when they Skype us!"

"They know perfectly well we're never going to do that."

"But Kenneth can be quite a nag, can't he?"

"And you can be quite the chatterbox. Good night."

"Oh, I'm just kidding. Let me take off all my clothes and throw them on the floor like the vile man I am, taking extra care to put my smelly socks on top of the pile . . . there . . . and hand me that hairbrush, if you'll be so kind."

She handed it to him. It was silver. Part of a vanity set that had belonged to her mother. No hair ever touched the bristles, which seemed misnamed, because they were as soft as down. He ran his fingers over them. It was a little gesture of warm-up, like a pianist stretching his fingers above a keyboard.

He held her foot in one hand, though she certainly had the strength to keep her foot in the air, but that was an old debate, and actually she was reassured by her total reliance on him. He placed the brush against the undersides of her toes and brushed down, slowly, only the first split second ever so slightly tickling; thereafter, she felt no such sensation. He brushed a hundred times, always stroking in the same direction, as if brushing hair. She trusted that he brushed her foot one hundred times because she'd long ago stopped counting. The stroking took away the ache in her elbow and the pain in her shoulder, and it dulled the pain behind her head, where the stitches had been taken against her will, after she tripped and fell. "Six stitches! They're nothing! Only the tiniest bit of hair had to be shaved, and the other hair lies on top of it." He'd held out the mirror, the silver mirror, which she'd taken in her hand but not been willing to look into, after turning her back to the mirror on the bureau. Now, as he stroked, she had a vision of the children when they were children: blurry and romanticized, not the crying, biting, pushy, and often wild-eyed creatures they'd been. They'd been one big snaggle, and in her worst moments she'd thought about how lovely it would be to just grab the clump of them and cut them out, no different than you'd cut out the unbrushable part of a dog's matted ruff, worth doing sometimes even with a hopelessly knotted little clump of your own hair. Though she hadn't. Only monstrous parents did that—or nowadays mothers put them in the car and drove into the water, eager to perish with them.

"Two hundred and six, two hundred and seven, two hundred and eight," he murmured. It was a lie. One hundred strokes was all he'd do, that was it, but if his joke contained a little protest, she imagined he must be nearing the end.

MISSED CALLS

Dear Mr. Cavassa: I received both your letters, the first be-
latedly because it was sent to my Virginia address and only
forwarded today. So my reluctance to talk about Truman
Capote isn't as great as you suspect in letter #2—just a problem of getting the mail at the right address. In #2 you say
that you are working with a former student of mine who
is digitalizing your archives. I remember Billie fondly and
hope she is still writing those wonderful, subversive little
vignettes. Your quote from Diane Arbus was wonderful (to
the effect that we can't despair, since we're all we've got).
I met her once, btw (as I now know to say), when I went to
a surprise party for Dick Avedon. Blowing up balloons with
her seemed easier than gushing admiration. Now, I wish
we'd talked—though that sort of imbalance rarely results
in anything long-lasting, in my experience. I was dating a
friend of Avedon's who took me to the party as a last-minute substitute when his mother developed a toothache. All

more than you want to know. Capote I hardly knew at all, so I doubt that a trip to Maine would benefit you—though it's not at all a question of my "finding time." When would you like to meet? With best wishes, Clair Levinson-Jones.

Dear Clair (if I may), Thank you for the quick reply. I'll be attending my goddaughter's graduation from Bowdoin in early June, and if you could see me on either side of that—the 5th or 7th would be ideal—I would be grateful for a little of your time. If you're so inclined, and there's somewhere you like to have lunch, it would be my pleasure to have a meal together. I do understand how busy you must be, however—so even a glass of water and a few moments of conversation will be fine! Thank you again for getting back to me so quickly. All best, Terry.

Terry—the 7th is good, though there may be some banging because of a new sink being installed in the upstairs bathroom. Tell me approximately what time to expect you, so I will not be running an errand. Again, I hope that my very few recollections about Capote are not a disappointment, but you've been warned! With best wishes, Clair.

Noon, Clair, so I might take you to lunch? Anticipating meeting with great pleasure. Best, T.

Terry—I will look for you about noon. Dockside is a restaurant near the water that I sometimes go to, though lunch tends to be a meal I forget. And breakfast consists mostly of vitamins. Though perhaps it would be good to have a bit of midday fuel. It is slightly tricky to find, so come to the house and we'll go together. Do you need any driving instructions? Best wishes, Clair.

My GPS should get me there. Until then, T. Anticipating with great pleasure.

Terry—I won't send this letter, though sometimes it's good to write something and tear it up, since the simplest things one wants to write just dissipate into words that sound good and have a logical configuration on the page, yet don't really communicate what I want to say. Do you already know that Capote visited us, and are you expecting his essence might be indelible, even if—assuming you're like other writers and photographers I know—you have no mystical beliefs? He peed in the toilet upstairs across from what will be the new pedestal sink. He may have done more than pee—that might be why he went upstairs, rather than using the downstairs half bath. Would it be amusing if I dithered aloud about this to you, a bit nervously, wanting to ingratiate myself, as the old do with the young? Or should I make an attempt to take your subject seriously and not conduct myself for my amusement? We must not talk of toilets at all, but of how good the fish chowder is, or how lovely the lobster salad (which I'll probably not order, since the days of lavish expense accounts are over). Chances are we'll never meet again but instead have some little flutter of follow-up on some minor point, and at Christmas I suppose you could astonish me by sending an unintentionally bizarre floral display with glittery pinecones protruding like enormous hatpins. My resentment of the young drips into everything I say, I fear—I, too, am a leaking sink. What it costs to install a sink nowadays! But I'll save that for hectoring the repairman. No one thinks Capote was a major talent any longer. Now everyone is a prodigy. No one even knows the names of the most serious contemporary writers unless they're local "celebs" who come out to eat organic cheese on hand-hewn toothpicks to benefit some do-good organization. I was once in a car when the GPS registered "CR" as CRESCENT, rather than CIRCLE. It turned out there was a CRESCENT (in New York State!) in some built-yesterday housing development, and there we were, the driver and me, at the wrong address for the B and B at nearly midnight. It's good you're Anticipating with great pleasure, because like all old people I fear the future (An' forward, tho' I canna see, I guess an' fear). The sound you hear is paper ripping, Terry of the genteel manners.

Adver had not come to install the new sink, just as she'd suspected he wouldn't. He had no phone. He was probably hungover. He often had the "flu." He would show up eventually, and she'd begun to enjoy brushing her teeth in the shower, so what did it matter? Better that the house be quiet for their conversation.

Across the street she saw the bushes, slightly greener than the day before. This intermediate stage was not her favorite. In certain light, she liked to photograph the tangled branches with the iPad, whose camera was the only one she had anymore. All of Demeter's things had been donated to the Maine College of Art, where he'd guest-lectured the last few years of his life. Eight days from diagnosis to death. No memorial service, as he'd requested. Instead, she'd bought half a dozen kites and given them to the front desk clerk, who handed them out to children staying at the Stage Neck Inn—the hotel right above the beach. She'd sat in the bar having a glass of wine with her friend Barb Gillicut, still in shock the weekend after Dem's death, watching the surprised children lean like cats stretching their paws on the thighs of their fathers, who prepared the kites to be sailed. Eventually a sumo wrestler flapped by with *Silence of the Lambs* teeth and contorted mightily in the wind before crashing to the sand. Unlike balloons, no kites simply drifted away as she watched, sharing a second glass of wine with Barb, aware that the bartender had her eye on them and was drying glasses like a Gypsy having a manic fit over a crystal ball, simultaneously polishing and trying to appear disinterested.

Dem was long dead. Dead for years and years. She herself was seventy-four. If he'd lived, he would have been eighty-eight. The Stage Neck now employed a female bartender, who therefore undoubtedly worried less about the mental state of other women. She picked up a crumpled bag in the road. Any car turning onto the street might be Terry in his rental car, which might be either white or red, as rental cars tended to be. All other cars were silver.

How had she ended up here? She was a Virginia girl. Virginia, where spring came a month and a half earlier than it did in southern Maine. In Virginia the problem was bees. In Maine, blackflies and mosquitoes. Well—the problem with bees now was that they were dying. It was a very bad situation.

One Dem would have worried about incessantly, pointing out every terrible thing that would arise due to the death of the bees. He would have made photographs of dead bees, and eventually—when the moon no longer appeared at night, or something equally dire—his photographs would be shown at MoMA. Eventually one would be sold at auction in New York City and a framed print of a dead bee would be hung above the marble-topped table of a discerning, socially correct, environmentally anxious couple in Park Slope, so they'd have an expensive little altar of sadness, the photograph taking the place of Christ on the cross, the table an old-fashioned, humble altar that sometimes might feature the perfect still life of our times (of course minus flowers or fruit): a key ring and a Binky and a bottle of Klonopin and an unopened Dasani water.

Red. An unpleasant maroon shade, like menstrual blood. Better, though, than a screaming fire-engine red. So many things going on in the car: a wave; a hand flipping the sun visor back into place; the side window rolling down, then rising again, finally all the way down to allow for an awkward first handshake. Terry wore rectangular glasses with heavy black frames that magnified his eyes and called attention to his facial asymmetry, one eye larger than the other. Brown eyes. Slightly thinning brown hair. Nervous hands: smoothing his hair, dropping the keys, snatching them up again, a sort of stammering dance in the driveway as he wondered aloud about locking the car. He reached back in for his notebook and cell phone, which he slid into the pocket of his sports coat.

She preceded him up the walkway, not wide enough

for two at a time (one of Dem's complaints). She imagined that Terry, behind her, was sneaking a last, quick look at the phone. A robin hopped across the lawn. There was a nest in the climbing rose.

"I confess, I've already been to Dockside," he said. "This is no way for us to begin, but I've just been through the most awful couple of days, and to be honest, my goddaughter's with me. At Dockside. I found out when I called for a lunch reservation that they rent rooms. She won't join us for lunch, of course, but she's there because . . . well, because her mother is acting far worse than Hannah, she has a frightful temper when things don't go her way. I do apologize for bursting out with what's troubling me, but it's left me quite disoriented, really."

She poured him a glass of Perrier. She poured one for herself. He didn't seem in any shape to question about ice or no ice, so she held out the glass. "What's happened?" she said. She'd feared he'd be some somber academician, but she suddenly realized that there was no reason to assume he taught. He was certainly voluble. Nothing to worry about there. A man Dem would have taken to instantly. When he was alive, she resisted his spontaneously formed likes and dislikes. Now that he was dead, she channeled his opinions.

"Leigh's inability to have any empathy whatsoever is hardly helpful in a bad situation. I'm so sorry. Of course you don't even know these people . . ."

Water wet his chin, he'd taken such a big gulp. He sat at the kitchen table without asking if he might. Which was fine. It was a little chilly on the back porch. There was a space heater, but she suddenly felt embarrassed that he might know she sat on the porch with a heater aimed at her. She pulled out a chair and sat across from him. She said, "I must admit, you've got me very interested."

"She hasn't graduated, is the thing. What I don't understand is that this failure to graduate came as no surprise to her, but why she let her mother and father arrange a celebration and book two rooms—Rand came from San Francisco with his girlfriend. Why Hannah didn't say something beforehand, I don't understand, though now she tells me they're intimidating. That her father roars at her. That was her exact word. Not the stereotype of someone who lives in San Francisco, is it? I understand that Leigh can be quite bullish. It's a crisis of some sort, that's obvious, and at the college there was absolutely no one to see about it. The dean couldn't meet with them at all yesterday because of her responsibilities at graduation. What we were all expected to do, other than sitting around the motel, I can't imagine. There was only one blessed time-out when everyone agreed not to discuss it and we had gelato. It was over in twenty minutes, then the accusations started again and the tears. Hannah seemed to have calmed down by the time she and I left. There's a boyfriend who's coming for her tonight, on the bus from Boston. He's premed. I'm awfully sorry to be dumping all this in your lap. I really must shut up."

"Not on my account. I don't get many visitors, let alone people who are caught up in a great drama. All I understand so far, though, is that for some reason this young woman didn't graduate."

"She didn't take any of her final exams! You'd think they'd get in touch with her, see if there was some reason for it.

Maybe they did try to contact her. I don't know. She called this Boston fellow her fiancé and Leigh acted like she'd said 'my shaman' or something. What if he is? Her fiancé, I mean. Not that I have the slightest idea what that would have to do with her not finishing her work."

"Have you spoken to him?"

"I don't know his name. I've never met anyone she's dated. She keeps that information top secret. You try to listen, to let them talk about what they're inclined to talk about, isn't that right? What do I know? I'm not a father."

"I'm not a mother, so I'm not the best person to give advice."

"I don't quite know how to handle it. Not that I know what 'it' is, if you'll excuse me for sounding like Bill Clinton. Leigh went absolutely berserk, pointing her finger at me, saying, 'You're so sympathetic, you figure this out, you support her so I'm not working two jobs.' She was exaggerating there. She has one part-time job, and I know for a fact that Rand gave her a very nice financial settlement. If she thinks of her volunteer work as a job, I suppose that's fair enough, but money's not a problem. Actually, she may have been a bit unnerved from the moment she met Rand's girlfriend, who plays with the San Francisco symphony. These aren't inherently strange people, a musician and a medical student. I do agree with Hannah that in this circumstance, Leigh's temper was quite terrible."

"The girlfriend's young?"

"She's thirtysomething. Leigh and I are both forty-eight. We met when I had my first job. We were guides in Colonial Williamsburg."

"Really? I grew up in Charlottesville."

"Ah, that's also a beautiful place. We drove there a few times for Leigh to see a shrink. She got pregnant by the candlemaker, during the time she was in love with the blacksmith. She couldn't decide what to do. I must say, back then when she leaned on me it was much easier to take than her finger pointed in my face like a witch, as though I shared any responsibility for this."

"So Hannah is the child of Leigh and a candlemaker?"

"No, that happened five years before she had Hannah. She had an abortion."

"I see. But her relationship with her daughter was good, you thought? Why do you think Hannah did what she did?"

"I'm not saying this to dodge the question, but I think I just don't understand women. I don't mean to disparage women. There's something I don't get. Me. That I, personally, don't get."

"But how can you understand them if they won't discuss the situation? The Perrier's on the top shelf, if you'd like more."

"Let's go to Dockside! I'm terribly sorry to have brought my problems to you. I'm entirely sure she's in her room, trying to figure things out, for all I know she's called her mother and apologized and everything's fine. I felt like Humbert Humbert checking in with her. The woman at the desk gave us such a skeptical look, even though I said two bedrooms and explained that she was my goddaughter. Hannah's eyes were red and almost swollen shut at that point, which the woman no doubt noticed. We both had to show our driver's licenses. I guess that's become routine. When you check in anywhere."

"I've heard that."

"Rand flew back home from Bangor. He's a surgeon. There was no way to stay. And the girlfriend couldn't miss another rehearsal. It was the first time she'd met Hannah, so what use could she be?"

"Are you using vacation time from your own job to make this trip, Terry? Which is a not very subtle way of asking what you do, I guess."

"What I do? I'm a writer, like you. I published a book in England about Emily Dickinson's neighbors. An expansion of my thesis. I majored in psychology at Brown, with a minor in American studies."

"Ah. Understanding psychology would be a prerequisite for writing about Mr. Capote, I should think."

"I'm not so much writing about him as about people who have negative effects on other people's lives. People are always writing about their mentors and thanking everyone they've ever met on the acknowledgments page. Everybody has wonderful, supportive, devoted people in their lives. All their pets are perfect. I think there needs to be another kind of book, a more realistic book, out there."

"I see. So how does Truman Capote fit into this?"

"Being responsible for Ann Woodward's suicide, for example. The woman who pretended she thought her husband was a burglar and shot him?"

"And now Pistorius. *Plus ça change.* But let me understand: you're writing a book about people who have adversely affected other people."

"I suppose that's it, in a nutshell. Other famous people, of course. America loves celebrity."

"Any small anecdote I might have about Capote isn't likely to justify your investment of time."

"At least you know who he is! When I reeled off some names to Hannah, she'd hardly heard of anybody—even though quite a few lived in Maine. She'd heard the name Truman Capote and she thought he wrote Christmas stories for children! She'd never heard of Diane Arbus, she'd never heard of Elizabeth Bishop. She'd heard of Robert Lowell, though she's never read anything by him. I suppose he isn't taught in school anymore."

"Cal—Lowell—was so much older than we were, but he was very kind to Dem. He wrote a letter that got him a Guggenheim when we badly needed money. That poem Elizabeth Bishop wrote after his death is one of the saddest things I've ever read. Will Lowell be in your book? Because of his negative effect on almost everyone?"

"Not on Bishop. They loved each other."

"That's true. So he's exempt?"

"Yes."

"You're serious? Being in love with one person is all it takes to get off the shit list?"

"I never considered including him. Phil Spector is in the book."

"I don't know who that is."

"Wall of Sound?"

"I'm afraid I have to let you down, just like Hannah."

"Not at all! It's very nice of you to make time for me. Please, let me take you to lunch. Hannah won't . . . she won't spring out from behind a bush, or anything. You know how they are. They want to be off by themselves to text and listen to their music and reapply all that makeup that doesn't look like makeup, and then they're exasperated if you suggest they put on some lipstick and comb their hair."

Clair got up and lifted her key ring from the nail by the door. She'd never changed the key ring; it was still the clunky little geode dangling from the end of a brass chain Dem had always carried, saying he'd gotten it from the Lilliputians, who swung it to knock out their Lilliputian enemies. Enemies. What a concept. Something people emphasized during wartime. Or that they still might call political opponents or predators in the animal kingdom. Down the street, the lawn service was unloading a riding mower. The violets would go under, and the dandelions with them. The service had pulled up where Adver's ex-wife lived—the woman he still sometimes dropped by to see after he made repairs. Those times he wasn't too hungover to make the repairs he'd promised to make. ("Just turn off the valve. I'll be there early Tuesday.")

"So you knew Lowell," Terry said. "I envy you that. Did you ever meet Elizabeth Hardwick?"

"I did. At a dinner in New York. I sat next to her and we talked about Trollope. Or she talked about him and I listened."

"That was one classy lady."

"She was. She had very curly hair and it kept blowing all through dinner, though there wasn't a fan anywhere. It just blew."

"How do you account for that?"

"Maybe her ideas, disturbing the currents of the air?"

"You're quite funny. I'm sure people tell you that."

"At my age, friends don't pronounce on other friends any

longer, and no one new I meet ever takes the slightest notice of me."

"Do you miss Virginia?"

"Particularly in April, when spring doesn't come here, and doesn't come."

"Blackflies do," he said.

"That's right. What about you? Do you miss it?"

She realized, now that the talk had turned banal, that earlier they'd been having a little flirtation. To no end, but they'd had an amusing volley. She touched her hair. She rubbed the tip of her nose, delicately. It never helped to scratch the itch in allergy season.

"I try not to miss places, because they're all so different now. Maybe not the heart of Williamsburg, but that's a sort of Disneyland, isn't it? Everything else changes."

"You're too young to think that way. You're supposed to see it as progress. Or not to notice at all."

"I'm a writer. I have to notice."

The waiter introduced himself. Michael was six feet tall, with blazing blue eyes. He recited the specials like a choirboy sight-reading complicated music for the first time. His eyes locked on the nothingness of the middle distance as he spoke. When he walked away in his white shirt and black pants, Clair saw that he was wearing yellow sneakers without laces. Had Terry, with the imperative to notice things, noticed that? They both ordered coffee.

Clair said, "I'll tell you my one Truman Capote story and get it over with, then you must tell me something you've discovered writing your new book. What you know will be far more interesting than anything I have to say, but here goes: I was friends with one of Johnny Carson's ex-wives, Joanne. She took a road trip with Capote to visit her sister, who lived just outside Charlottesville, but her sister suddenly came down with what turned out to be mumps so they ended up staying with me for a night. Dem wasn't famous then. He and I were housesitting for some university couple who'd gone to Spain, taking care of their garden and feeding their cat. I cooked a chicken and made a salad. I wasn't going to a lot of trouble just because the famous Truman Capote was coming to dinner. He'd like me or he wouldn't. Dem always said one of the things that attracted him to me was my self-assurance. Anyway, to my surprise, he was rather shy. He kept calling some friend named Leo on the telephone and leaving dollar bills 'for the phone bill.' Maybe ten dollars. When he was leaving, he reminded me that the money was by the phone and said that if I wanted, he'd sign his name on the bills. Can you imagine? Sometimes people say things like that to test you: how impressed are you that they've been in your house? Did I say Dem was away on an assignment? I said something like 'Do whatever you think best,' and he hesitated, then walked back to the kitchen. We stood there while he autographed dollar bills. Joanne was rolling her eyes, but she adored him. She thought everything he did was amusing. After they left, I saw that all the signatures were different. They all said Truman Capote, but some of the writing was slanted backward, and some of it looked like calligraphy, and in one the *T* had curlicues at the top like ram's ears. If I still had them, I might be able to list them on eBay. He also guessed almost to the penny what the phone bill would be."

"I've never heard anything like that. He wasn't drunk?"

"We shared the bottle of wine Joanne brought, but three people on a bottle of wine? No, hardly drunk. He slept on the couch and she slept in the other twin bed in the room Demeter and I shared. In the morning when we got up he was playing with the cat."

"Were you tempted to keep the money?"

"It was money. I spent it."

"That was the only time you ever saw him?"

"He came one other time to the house in Maine right after we moved in, but he obviously didn't remember meeting me in Virginia. Either that, or I'd changed more than I realized. We never want to think that, do we? I'd had long hair when we first met—another thing Dem said he'd loved about me, at first sight—but by the time I saw Truman Capote again, I'd had it cut. I was just Demeter Farrell's middle-aged wife. He looked right through me, even when he asked in that whispery voice where the loo was. I pointed and he hesitated. He sort of lingered in the kitchen as the others went out to the back porch—there'd been talk of his writing something about Demeter's new show for the *New Yorker*—and then he set down his iced tea, I think it was. He turned his back on me and walked upstairs, where he must have known there'd be another bathroom, and he used that one instead. That's the end of my Truman Capote stories. Now they're yours!"

"What did you think of someone coming in and accepting your hospitality and basically brushing you off?"

"I was only the famous photographer's wife."

"Would women have treated you that way?"

"Most all our visitors were men."

"But you mentioned Diane Arbus in your letter."

"Her daughter went to school in Maine. She built her own yurt to live in. She loved her school. Diane was skeptical of how much education she was getting, but she was glad Amy—that was her name—had found a place she felt she belonged. Diane Arbus certainly didn't autograph anything before leaving!"

"Didn't May Sarton also live in York?"

"She did, and we went out of our way to avoid her. She was a very contentious person."

"I'm obviously lucky you agreed to see me! Here comes the coffee, finally. They aren't in any hurry here, are they? Just meeting you has put my mind back on my project. What a strange story about Capote, though. Do you think he mistook himself for Picasso and thought anything could be his merely for signing a napkin?"

"See the man coming in, in the Boston Whaler? Diane Arbus should be here. He used to be Karen Welber. Had surgery at Johns Hopkins. Ken's been married for thirty years to a German girl who doesn't speak a word of English, or pretends she doesn't. She pantomimes to the butcher how she wants the meat prepared. The butcher hates it when she comes in."

"Is that right? Really?"

"Yes. There's also a midget who lives in town."

"But you like it here? You haven't thought about getting away for the winter, at least? Florida's not for you?"

"Not for me, no."

"Some dependable people who shovel you out? All that?"

"I haven't had any trouble doing the walkway and the steps myself, and if Adver isn't too drunk or hungover, he gets to my driveway quite fast, since his ex lives on the same street and would kill him if he didn't drive the plow over before the snow stopped falling."

"Your husband did a different sort of photography, of course, but did he . . . for his own purposes, I mean—did he photograph people in town? Landscapes? Anything like that?"

"A lot of nude shots of me, but no landscapes, no."

"Oh, I see!"

"I was kidding."

"Oh! Right!"

He blushed! She'd made him blush!

"What exactly are your plans when your young friend's fiancé comes on the bus, Terry? Hadn't you better check on Hannah's state of mind? Everyone seems to have ditched you with a twenty-one-year-old girl. I've never heard of anything like that."

"I know what you mean. I'm feeling a bit sorry for myself, like I've got to see that this comes to some good conclusion, even though it's not really my responsibility."

"It's none of my business, but when you were younger, were you Hannah's mother's boyfriend? I couldn't make that out from the way you told the story."

"Well, I—I don't really know if I was. I mean, at the time I thought I was, or at least that that might happen any moment. She always had her various unhappy romances going on. But we had something special, I know we had that. It was probably just wishful thinking on my part that there would be anything more. You know, I don't tend to talk about her. No one's ever asked me that."

"Your being her daughter's godfather, and your long friendship . . ."

"Oh, perfectly logical question, exactly right. I don't think I knew quite what to do. I didn't want to ruin the friendship, I suppose. So I never did anything—anything that a real boyfriend would do, I mean—though sex alone doesn't account for closeness, does it?"

"As you mentioned earlier: Bishop and Lowell."

"Exactly. Perfect example. They had so much in common and they were so much on each other's side. Really quite remarkable, that friendship. And then at the very end, you have to wonder what he was thinking when he was going to visit her here. Here being Maine, I mean. He meant to bring Mary McCarthy along, and Elizabeth Bishop was living with a woman, and she didn't want Mary McCarthy to see that, or whatever it was she feared, so Lowell didn't come. It was obtuse of him, really stupid. They never saw each other again. It would have been the last visit. It's really too sad to think about."

"That isn't Hannah down there throwing rocks in the water, is it?"

"It is Hannah. My god! I didn't even see her crouched down there. I've known her since she was four days old. Yet you never know another person, do you? That's the old cliché, at least. She's always been willful. She's always felt her way is the right way. What a strange feeling to be spying on her from afar. Sometimes when they're that age you feel like they're performing for you, but that's not what we're seeing."

"No. She has no idea we're watching."

"Look what she's doing. It's like tossing coins in a fountain. She's wishing for good luck, whatever that might mean to her. I don't see why they didn't try to find out at least what she was thinking, or if she was suffering in some way. They've left it to me, you're right. Not the sort of parents I'd want to have. Where did she get all those stones?"

"She's filled her pockets like Virginia Woolf. She probably scooped them up from the parking lot."

He frowned into his empty coffee cup. They had not been offered refills. "Let's hope she's not that disturbed by anything," he said.

"What time does the bus come in?"

"She hasn't told me. There was some question about whether he could get here in time for dinner, or whether she and I should eat alone."

"You could call her and ask if it's been decided."

"You wouldn't mind? I find it so rude when—"

"Also, Terry, to put you at ease: I know my little stories aren't anything that can help you. You won't disappoint me if I read the book and they aren't in it. There were interviews with Dem—interviewers who came, who asked questions for days, and we knew that the longer someone asks questions, the more likely it is that very little of what you say will appear in print. Dem and I both felt that."

"That the sense of the person would be lost, rather than discovered, do you mean?"

"Exactly."

"You know, I'm really going to try to work in the story about signing the money. Everyone likes to read about peculiar actions. Especially ones that aren't hugely significant. Ones that don't sum everything up, I mean. Things that just happened because they happened."

A stone glinted in the sunlight before plunking into the water where boats bobbed on their moorings. Hannah's hair was flaxen. It was wavy and thick and caught the light like a yellow, shot-silk curtain. Part of it was gathered back, but the rest was an unruly, gorgeous mess of blond hair. It overpowered everything, including her slim body.

"I won't take offense if you call her before our lunch arrives."

"All right, then," he said, taking his phone out of his pocket.

He scrolled quickly to find her number, but when his thumb pressed the button, he used enough force to push it through the phone. The expression on his face as the phone rang and rang—turned off? Or was she willfully not answering?—was dolorous, filled with intense sorrow in the second before he remembered where he was and raised his eyes and shrugged his feigned dismissal. Then, almost instantly, he turned his head and narrowed his eyes, staring into the distance. Clair glanced quickly over her shoulder to see what he was seeing. It was the waiter, approaching with a huge circular tray. The young man had no more idea how to carry the tray aloft than a blind man would know how to proceed if handed an Olympic torch.

Behind Terry's ear—at the spot where photographers told you to focus when they made your portrait so you wouldn't gaze too intently into the lens (which paradoxically made your expression silly, rather than intense), the long-haired Hannah suddenly tossed what turned out to be her last few pebbles into the water, as if they'd been burning her palm. But she was young, and her dramatic moment was over. Next, she withdrew her phone from her pocket, though to Clair's surprise that, too, was thrown in the air as if it were a hot coal. It flew in a steep arc across the water until it sank. She'd done it so impulsively. Or might she have sensed that she was being observed? It had been Dem's opinion that you could always sense the photographer's presence in a great photograph— though he also believed that sometimes what you were seeing was the moment the photographer actually turned his back on what he was seeing, so the image became a record of the photographer's exit. Terry had a problem on his hands, as he must know. Hannah stood at water's edge, her bowed head that of a penitent. If she had it to do over again, would she?

THE REPURPOSED BARN

"There are Elvis lamps at the auction," Bettina said. "Also a collection of reptile purses. What do you suppose those are? I assume, alligator bags? There's a parlor set, which you can bet is so out of fashion it won't meet the minimum bid, which is fifty-five dollars. You couldn't get two mani-pedis for that. Get this: there's no minimum on 'assorted kitchen implements from Italy,' including brass measuring cups whose description is written out in Italian, so I can't make any sense of it, and a chestnut-handle pizza cutter."

Jocelyn's mother and—beyond belief!—her boyfriend, Nick, were driving to Maine on Friday and would stay for the weekend at a motel (they had to have that much sex?) and take Jocelyn back with them to the house the bank hadn't yet repossessed. He'd moved in. Her mother had been seeing this man for almost a year and had never once mentioned him? How was that possible, when her mother was home every night and hardly ever got a phone call? She was lying;

she'd just met him. You just had to assume adults lied. Why not say she'd just met the guy? Nobody was going to faint if somebody old had a boyfriend. They were feeling each other up in nursing homes, steering their wheelchairs into each other's to flirt! Ancient people who ran around the halls at night, jumping into each other's beds. (She'd found this out during the summer from Zelda's mother, who was a health aide and who would discuss really gross topics.) The one incentive to go to college was to get out of the house, which she still thought they might lose, because she'd overheard so many of her uncle's phone calls and he never seemed reassured by them. It would even be better to continue living where she was—her uncle was a nice man now that he was no longer doing gross things for the government, and Bettina was definitely better after she was discharged from the hospital and stopped cramming food down her throat day and night. Jocelyn would have to go with her mother, but she'd be counting the days until she could be on her own. Angie had asked her mother if Jocelyn could live with them, and she'd said certainly not, she had a mother. If that was the kind of logic she was up against, then no: there was no one to save her. She wasn't going to give the Nick person the satisfaction of banishing her.

Her uncle was shocked by the Big News; he'd phoned her mother way too many times since he found out about her changed situation. Maybe he was warming up to have a heart attack. Somehow he'd been arranging the refinancing of his sister's house—then this! So where did Raleigh get the money, if neither of them had jobs? Though they tried to keep the information from her, she knew from overhearing

Bettina talking to Raleigh at night that one of their credit cards had been canceled, which made Bettina even more haywire about money. Bettina said it would be fun to go to the auction because she'd limit herself to twenty dollars— he could keep it in his pocket; she wouldn't even bring her purse—and anyway, it would be a pretty drive out into the country and they didn't just want to sit around and be sad that Jocelyn was leaving. Bettina could be really smarmy when she decided to try to appear brave and heroic; actually, she was guilt-tripping you. They were sad that her mother had picked up some stupid guy and let him move into the refinanced house, that was what they were sad about. They never talked about their own daughter, never said the words Charlotte Octavia (who'd been named for E. B. White's spider). Charlotte Octavia was living with her boyfriend L'il Co!MOTION in Seattle—and for that, she envied her.

Earlier that day her uncle had met with her teacher because (1) the bitch—which she turned out to be—was insisting that she rewrite the essay she hadn't given a passing grade to or she wouldn't graduate, and (2) he couldn't understand why her grades alternated between Cs and Ds, since it seemed clear to him that her essays had improved. He had no sympathy for her dragging her feet about the final essay, though Jocelyn knew that he thought Ms. Nementhal hadn't done a good enough job, if—according to her—Jocelyn's essays never improved, but wasn't it the teacher's fault if she didn't learn how to make them better? Aunt Bettina had made the appointment to talk to Ms. Nementhal; then, feigning dizziness, she'd sent Raleigh in her place. If she'd really been dizzy, it was because of what she'd just found out about her sister-in-law, who was having sex way too soon after a hyster-ectomy. Her mother had insisted on a time-out, no texting or calls while she was recovering and Jocelyn was in summer school, and now it was clear why that served her purposes so well. Who wanted to be interrupted having sex?

Bettina had gotten her own message and called Raleigh in the middle of his golf game, in tears. Her uncle had turned into an instant liar—though he hadn't cut his golf game short. "I'm sure she's got a good reason for having a relation-ship with him," he'd said to Bettina as he came through the front door. "People have reasons we can't always understand, but if we have faith—"

"Stop rationalizing!" Bettina shrieked. "She told me he'd completed a drug rehab program."

"Well, for a time I was in AA," he said. "You don't hold that against me."

"That has nothing to do with this," Bettina said. "He was a landlord in New York City, and he lost his entire building, including his own apartment, and when he met her he was staying on a friend's foldout couch in Queens, engaged to another one of the addicts."

Raleigh winced. "We shouldn't be discussing this in front of Jocelyn," he said. "Another time, maybe you can tell me how you know that."

"Another time, I'll try to jump-start your brain, Raleigh."

"I'm going to Angie's to write my essay," she said. "Is ev-erybody okay with that, or would you like me to send flowers and a note of congratulations to Mom?"

"What if you grow up and you're as ignorant as you are right this minute?" Bettina said. She answered herself: "Then it's heredity, I suppose, and we can pity you. You're not going to her house to write any essay. You'll go down to the beach and smoke pot, or whatever you do. Probably hatch a plan to murder your teacher, or something that will ruin your life, as if your mother hasn't done enough! What good did that shrink do her, I want to know. Maybe she met the drug addict in his waiting room."

"We really aren't the kind of people who talk this way, are we, Bettina? As if we're better than people who address their problems?" Raleigh ran his hands through his hair. He said, "I think this news just has to settle in."

"And when it's settled in and bored a hole in your heart, what then?"

"It's so pointless! You're not going to be able to do anything about it!" Jocelyn said. "Do you think what you say matters? Do you?"

"This is very distressing," Raleigh said. "We can only hope we've got the story wrong."

Jocelyn noticed that his limp was more pronounced as it got later in the day. He went to the best chair and sat down.

"This is what people's children put them through, not their sisters," Bettina said. "This is bad for my health. You're right. Let her mess up her life, but we've got to look out for Jocelyn." There it was again! The noble, passive-aggressive bullshit.

"Like how?" Jocelyn said. "Adopt me? Go deeper into debt to send me to college so I can make Cs and Ds?"

"Your teacher has a strange perspective on what an essay should be," Raleigh said. "I shouldn't say this, but she referred me to an essay by Flannery O'Connor about peacocks.

Let her admire whatever she wants, but this essay is no masterpiece, let me tell you. It's slightly witty, but she goes on and on about some peacock walking around in her front yard."

Jocelyn burst into tears. "Summer school was just about farming me out so she could have a good time," she said.

"Let's not give up hope," Raleigh said. "Let's drive to Myrtis's and see her and try to talk this through. I think that's what we should do tonight."

"Why?" Jocelyn said. "She doesn't want to see us, she wants to be with the drug addict."

"Please don't cause us more heartache," Bettina said. "Jocelyn, if you go over to Angie's, I want you to promise we won't get a call from the police telling us you're smoking pot at the beach."

"I don't do that! I don't use drugs! How many times do I have to tell you?"

"Would we all like to go out and get some ice cream?" Raleigh said.

"Go out, in this state? I wasn't this upset when they carried me away on a stretcher."

"Why don't you go upstairs and lie down then, Bettina?" He turned to Jocelyn. He was looking at her, but she could tell he didn't see her. "Do you—" His voice broke. "Maybe we could all go to that auction," he said. "It's like some reality show is going on in the living room. I feel like I've become a raving idiot in my own house. Worse things than this happen all the time. And don't ask me what they are."

Bettina whirled around and walked out of the room. The kitchen door did not slam shut because it was a swinging door. Water ran in the sink. Jocelyn looked at her uncle and his eyes met hers. Somehow, the worst of the spell had been broken. Jocelyn felt like vomiting. She went to the sofa and stretched out, kicking off her flip-flops. "Why did this have to happen?" she said. "I don't want to see her. I don't. And can you even imagine being in that man's presence?" Raleigh said nothing. She could hear him breathing deeply. She said, "I don't even care if you were CIA and she was the Torturer and you're hiding yourselves like Nazis in Maine and don't know anybody, because, okay, you know a couple of people, but basically you don't know anybody. It's really obvious."

"I'm afraid I don't understand one thing you just said, Jocelyn."

"No?"

"Did you mean that we had no friends?"

Now it sounded stupid. Before the golf game, one of his golf buddies had come in for an iced tea. That same morning, someone named Hedda Rae, or something like that, had called to invite them to dinner, and Bettina had lied her way out of it. She admitted she had. "I can't spend an evening with somebody that boring," she'd said. Still, Jocelyn thought there was essential truth to what she'd said about their isolation. Truthiness, as Colbert would say. Colbert, who was selling out. How could he? But you weren't supposed to think about individuals, you were supposed to worry about the planet. The Earth was so fucked. She went into the bathroom and tried to choke up something that wasn't quite in her stomach, but not in her throat, either. She splashed cold water on her face. She felt horrible.

Music? When she went back to the living room, Raleigh was standing with his hands in his pockets, jingling change and listening to music: more classical sludge, like whale shit, seen blurrily underwater. Hey—that was pretty good! She gave herself a thumbs-up with her yet-again-gnawed cuticle and sank back into the sofa. Her uncle stood with his back to her, looking out the window.

"Will anyone come with me to the auction?" Bettina said. She must have gotten different clothes from the laundry room adjacent to the kitchen. Her baggy slacks were wrinkled, but earlier she'd been wearing a skirt. The T-shirt was also different: dark blue, which accentuated her blue eyes. Raleigh looked blankly at his wife. "Sure," he said quietly, shrugging. "What about you, Jocelyn?"

This was what was happening? They were going to go to some stupid auction and try to distract themselves, when he no doubt wanted to have a drink and Bettina probably wanted to eat an extra-large pizza? They were so old, so worried all the time, though they tried to make it appear they were in control. "I'll go," she heard someone say. She was the one who'd said it.

"Good," Raleigh said. Her aunt said nothing. She picked up the section of newspaper that gave the address of the auction. "We would've been able to inspect things for the last half hour, and what have we done but miss our great opportunity?" Bettina said.

Jocelyn and Raleigh, avoiding looking at each other, got their jackets from the coat hooks in the hallway. In Maine, you learned to always carry a jacket, no matter how warm the evening—and shuffled out of the house with Bettina behind them, making sure the door was locked, pulling the handle three times. It was a signature gesture, as Angie would say.

One of Angie's mother's signature gestures was to put her face in her hands and cry for several seconds, after which she'd stop abruptly, take eye drops out of her pocket, and tilt her head back, flooding her face with liquid. The day before, Angie had also let drop a convincing detail about her make-out moment with T. G. She said one of her earrings had gotten caught in his arm hair, and she'd cried out, and he'd stopped immediately. Oh god. It was all so ordinary. There was no discharge date for T. G. that her uncle knew. She'd asked him that morning. The youngest son, Ted, was bouncing off the walls, and the parents were going to cave and let him be put on meds, they were so stressed out.

"The Queen Anne's lace is blooming," Bettina said. She turned to Jocelyn, who sat curled in the backseat with her legs tucked to one side. "They often have a little black insect right in the center," Bettina said. "Did you know that?"

Did I know I was fucked? Jocelyn wondered, re-forming the question. She lied about having noticed the flowers; she nodded yes, but Bettina rushed on, wanting to overwhelm everyone with how much information she had. She said, "And roses attract Japanese beetles. That's something everyone knows."

The sky was starting to darken. What would it be like to have her own car, to already have been through college? What would it be like to live in Seattle, where you could go on hikes and not always be sitting around some living room, being miserable?

Bettina told Raleigh he was about to miss his turn, and he said, "Sorry about that. Right."

When they got to South Berwick, Bettina showed him the

map. He said the auction was right where he thought it was. The road had potholes that made Jocelyn a little sick to her stomach, but she was feeling better, which was good, because it would have been really bad to feel worse. An auction. She wished it was a movie. She was the only person who hadn't seen the 3-D movie. Or it would be great if she'd been able to go to a play. Imagine seeing real actors, instead of having to sit for hours watching that kid Emmet Thornton, who lisped, playing Puck? That guy who'd OD'd—the actor in New York. It would have been great to see him in something before he died, though he wasn't cute. He looked like one of those big-headed dolls people put on their dashboards to wobble their heads. He'd been a father. He had kids who lived with the mother.

They passed Dunkin' Donuts and followed the road to where it turned at the bend. She'd never been to an auction. In spite of what her aunt had said, her purse was in her lap. She heard her unzip it and take out her glasses to look at the map a second time, then put them away.

"Here we go," Raleigh said, turning onto a lawn where a teenager with a white flag waved him forward. They bounced through deep ruts, Raleigh holding the wheel tightly in both hands. "Ridiculous," he muttered. "What do we get for our tax dollars?" Another car in front of them bumped into a parking place, and Raleigh turned in beside it. "Close up the hole!" the boy said, pointing his flag at the other car.

"There's about three inches between us," Raleigh said, rolling down the window. "If I parked closer, we wouldn't be able to get out." He put his window up again. "Idiot," he said, under his breath. The boy had walked away and was waving his flag at the next car.

"Are we going to get the parlor set for Jocelyn? And keep it as her dowry?" Bettina asked Raleigh, but he was walking too far ahead of her to hear. Jocelyn slapped a mosquito that was either trying to or had succeeded in biting her ear. "Shit!" she said. "Language," her aunt said. A young man and his blond girlfriend walked through the space between Jocelyn and Bettina, hurrying across the field toward the auction barn. They joined hands once they'd passed by, and the girl flipped her long blond hair over her shoulder. "Alex!" someone shouted. "Hey, Alex, you've got to come see our puppies!"

Alex hollered, "Hey—you don't care that my mom's moved to London? You think I care about your puppies? I'm one of those puppies now!"

"What?" the girl said. "Where did she go?"

"She rode off on a coach like Cinderella, only it was C & J. Next auction, we can clean out her room and make money! My dad would totally appreciate help in emptying the house!"

Jocelyn killed two more mosquitoes before they got to the barn, and Bettina gripped the thick handle of her big purse. Jocelyn had rummaged in the purse, but only when her aunt told her to; she wasn't a creep like some kids who were always stealing money. She'd opened it to get Bettina a Kleenex when she was driving, to see if her lipstick was in there, to fish around for quarters for parking. The purse was nothing but a bag of disappointments. It was stupid to carry things like that. Only old people did it. To the side of the building was a concession stand, and Jocelyn thought, meanly, that if Bettina hadn't made it clear to her that she shouldn't spend money on things like overpriced Coke, she'd like one. Her mouth felt tingly; if she tried to throw up now, she'd probably be able to. A big man whose leg had been amputated above the knee rolled himself along, a bright yellow fingerless glove on one hand. The American flag dangled from a pole attached to the back. He wore one slip-on shoe and a black sock. You could see his stomach where his shirt was missing buttons. A little girl was tugging her mother's hand. "Stop it!" her mother said, pulling her along. "You behave."

"Hear that? That's the warning women have gotten through the ages, isn't it?"

Jocelyn didn't answer. Inside, the space was divided into two sections with a low wood fence blocking off the area where the auction items were on display. You could tell from a distance that nothing was very special. The building smelled of hay and mildew. Metal chairs were set up in rows. Right now, it looked easy to get a seat near the front. A man came in with a cane, and another man tried to strike up a conversation. The first man kept poking the cane tip toward the closed-off area. Finally he walked away and left the other guy talking to himself, cigarette cupped in his hand. The amputee rolled himself in front of all the chairs and put on his brake. A ceiling fan blew the flag, but otherwise little air circulated in the barn. Why couldn't they be at a movie? A vampire movie? The mother and child she'd seen earlier moved around the fence and looked but didn't enter, as if standing behind a rope, waiting for a bouncer to wave them in. One night she'd gone with her friend back home, Rachel, to a disco, but they'd never made it in, and finally they'd gone to a diner and split a foot-long hot dog. Rachel had a bottle of scotch in the car, but of course they couldn't bring that in.

Wouldn't it be great not to be carded and to be able to afford to eat and drink in a restaurant?

Inside, amid the clutter of tables and chairs and equipment and bolts of upholstery fabric, a lot of people were taking notes or laughing and talking to one another. At a card table near the back, a woman had you fill out a form attached to a clipboard. For a second, Jocelyn remembered her aunt's flip-out at the eye doctor's. At least there had been a medical reason for it. Her mother was just plain crazy. The woman handed out white cards with big numbers written on them with black Magic Marker when you returned the form. The girl Jocelyn had seen earlier—Alex?—was fanning her face with her card while her boyfriend rummaged through tool boxes. He was black-haired, with a tattoo of a rifle piercing a skull on his bulging bicep and sagging pants. He wore unlaced red high-tops. "You gonna bid on the King?" the woman sitting behind the card table asked the guy wearing a cowboy hat, who was standing in front of Alex and her boyfriend. "They all came out of the same house, which I heard belonged to the ex-husband of Lisa Marie Presley!" she said. "Her mother, Priscilla, got to be married to the King, and she ran off with the yoga instructor!"

"Well now, you slept with the King, yourself, in Las Vegas, didn't you? Wasn't that what you was telling me the other night, about all that hot sex?"

"Go on!" the woman said, laughing, handing him number 38. "One thing's for sure, and you're the living proof of it: we won't see the likes of him again."

"There it is! Look!" Bettina said. "Such beautiful green velvet. And notice the delicate carving on the wood. I believe it's a real Eastlake parlor set. We should get it for you, Jocelyn."

"I don't want that shit," Jocelyn said.

"Language," her aunt said halfheartedly, walking off to get a number.

"I'll bet you're sorry we came," Jocelyn said to Raleigh. "But hey: it's a distraction, right? We can try to forget the Nick scumbag exists. And it's what Bettina wanted to do."

"That's true," he said. "It pleases Bettina. She grew up in Michigan, you know, with her grandfather and grandmother. Her grandmother taught her to love old furniture."

Raleigh stuck out as not belonging in this crowd. She hoped she did, too. Bettina fit right in. She waved her number at Jocelyn and began to inspect the things close to where she'd gotten her bidding card. Jocelyn hung back, making sure to keep a distance between herself and her uncle. "Loving you, loving you!" the cowboy sang, gesturing toward a dozen or so Elvis lamps, hand over his heart as if he were saying the Pledge of Allegiance. The lamps had no shades. All of them—and there were a lot—were arranged on a long table. A few lampshades lay on the ground behind it. A small bird sat on top of one; it took off quickly toward the top of the barn when people approached. "Light switches work? Can we get some of those Dairy Queen swirled ice cream lookin', energy-savin' lightbulbs to come out of the King's head like snakes do you think?" Cowboy asked.

"I'm going to sit down," she said to Raleigh. He'd been watching the man who was infatuated with his own voice. He nodded. She took a chair five rows back from the podium, trying to ignore the man in the wheelchair, but the flag kept

drawing her attention. She closed her eyes and tried to remember the beach, Cassiopeia, the stars, how really black the
sky could be. Her one little thing with T. G., after which Zelda
arrived and acted really pissed off about something. Who
knew what. That they were sitting in the sand holding hands,
just the two of them? Big deal. When she opened her eyes,
the guy with the tattoos was pulling out a chair on the opposite side of the aisle, though the girl he'd been with never
did join him. Jocelyn stared, more or less because she didn't
know where else to look. The image of the rifle that curved
because of the way his muscle bulged was sort of riveting. BLT
kept rising up on her toes, trying to wave her over. Jocelyn
just wanted the auction to be over. In school, she wanted class
to be over. On the beach, she wanted to be back in her room.
In her room, she wanted to be in her house—her mother's
house. What was that going to be like, sharing space—sharing
her mother—with the drug addict?

She slid back farther in the chair, her butt already numb
from the metal. As she shifted her weight, she looked over
her shoulder and saw her. Ms. Nementhal was several rows
back, talking to a pretty woman. She saw her in profile, but
Ms. Nementhal didn't realize she'd been seen. She was busily
conversing. She brushed her hair out of her eyes and, with
the same hand, slid her arm around the woman's shoulder.
The woman looked at her with a little wry smile, her mouth
lipsticked red. It was one of those mouths that seemed to
have been delicately placed on someone's face, like a flower
tucked into a lapel. Jocelyn felt a jolt. A real jolt, like what it
must feel like to be hit by lightning. That was an exaggeration. It was a tingle, and a simultaneous numbness—so that

her butt wasn't the only thing without feeling. She got it. She absolutely got it. But what were they doing at this stupid auction in the middle of nowhere? How could it be? What could she do to make sure Ms. Nementhal didn't see her, since she was supposed to be writing her stupid fucking essay? Well, but wasn't Ms. Nementhal supposed to be preparing for the next day's class?

People seated around her immediately turned toward the fenced-off area as the lights suddenly dimmed and the Elvis lamps started flashing. Somehow, the bulbs were turning on and off in unison, the retarded cowboy singing another song and flipping a light switch, or using a remote, or whatever he held that made them flash. He was gyrating and singing "Jailhouse Rock." It was a pretty good imitation. It really was. Her uncle stood there, clapping his hands above his head.

She patted the seat next to her when Bettina appeared at her side. It wasn't likely, but maybe, maybe she could get out without Ms. Nementhal seeing her. Was she going to say anything about that to her aunt? No, she wasn't. In a few minutes Raleigh came and sat next to them, stepping over their legs to get to the third seat. Bettina was chattering away, obsessed with her parlor set. "Is it like something you've seen before?" Jocelyn said, just to be polite and to have something to say. "What do you think I've been saying to you the last five minutes? Do you listen at all? It's Victorian. It's almost the exact duplicate of the one my grandparents had when I was much younger than you, if it had rose-colored velvet instead of green!"

The auctioneer took the stand, two younger men with their arms dangling at their sides, wearing overalls, flanking him. He greeted the man in the wheelchair by name, though Jocelyn couldn't hear what he said. The yellow-gloved hand went into the air to make a gesture somewhere between hello and dismissal. After saying something to the auctioneer, the man started coughing. One of the auctioneer's assistants looked at him nervously. The coughing went on for quite some time. Then the auctioneer introduced himself: "The auctioneer who needs no introduction! The warm-up act for Mr. Elvis Presley!" He started to speak into the microphone, a maddening, jammed-up sequence of words that crashed like bumper cars, after which everything sorted itself into some kind of sense again, and after the fact you could understand most of what he'd said. He held the microphone like a Popsicle that had started to melt. The words tumbled over each other, the sounds dipping and rising. He joked that people were there for "the head of Elvis," but that he was going to offer sacrifices galore before they got to "the main body of the auction." He stood behind a rickety podium. The men at his sides stared straight ahead over the crowd, shoulders back, feet a certain distance apart, hands clasped behind them like soldiers at ease. One of the things Jocelyn remembered about her father was that he'd shown her the positions soldiers took: attention, at ease. She'd liked to stand beside him and copy whatever he was doing. Now, she thought that was an unfortunate thing about men: they were always posturing when they were young, and if they went into the Army, they taught them not only postures but attitude. Like guys needed more attitude.

The assistants only cracked up once, when the auctioneer tried to pronounce a lot of words she finally realized must be

199

Italian. They punched him in his arms and one went down on his knees and raised his arms to the barn roof, in some exaggerated, silent prayer. You could read his mind and understand basically what he was praying for. A lot of people laughed. "And who's gonna bid, who starts the bid, who'll give me fif-ty dollars?" he said, holding up an old doll whose hair was a mess, wearing only a top, no bottom. "And who says forty, over there: thirty-five? How can you be so pretty and be so mean? Do I hear thirty, what about twenty? She's got to go to a good home, who'll give me a quarter? Over there. And fifty cents? Thank you kindly. Seventy-five. Who'll go a dollar? Try to buy yourself a hot dog now for only one dollar! If you've been to Fenway Park, you'll know they cost five times that, am I right? Next year, mustard's sure to be extra! We're talking small potatoes here, folks, but don't break my heart and make me think I'm sellin' potato chips! I see a dollar. There and there, thank you, ma'am, and now we're at one dollar twenty-five cents. Look at this lovely dolly. Looks to me like she might need a good home. Brush her hair and she's good to go. One fifty. And one seventy-five. Going once, twice, one dollar and seventy-five cents? Number sixteen."

Half an hour passed while he sold one piece of junk after another: Crock-Pots, vacuum cleaners, a mirror frame with broken glass held in place with duct tape, a pair of stilts, a board game said to have all the pieces. Things kept going for fifty cents or a dollar. The auctioneer held up what he said were "cast-iron elephant bookends. They say an elephant never forgets, ain't that right, boys? Well, if it's only half an elephant I guess it's already forgotten half its body, but give me your finest bid. Who's in at thirty dollars? Is that a bid? Twenty-five for these fine elephant fellows, or maybe it's Mr. and Mrs. and eventually that might get you a third elephant. What will you bid? One dollar? And two! Two fifty! And three! Now we're rollin'. Four dollars. Don't quit on me now. Four it is, thank you kindly. And five. The lady with the pink sweater. Five dollars I've got, now six. Six? Going for five dollars? Number forty-nine!"

The lights dimmed and the Elvis busts flashed again, though this time some lit up while others stayed off, and for at least the third time, the guy in the cowboy hat did his Elvis impersonation, singing with the microphone almost in his mouth, wiggling his hips and unzipping his fly for a grand finale. You couldn't see anything. Not even his underwear. Bettina was startled. She reached for Raleigh's hand, and he took hers, but he was grinning and didn't look at her. He didn't want to miss anything.

The Elvis lamps, held up one by one beside the auctioneer as he took bids, did better than anything that preceded them. A man in a tweed jacket one row up rarely lowered his number. Eventually both other bidders dropped away. He didn't bid on a few of the lamps, but the rest of the time he held his card steady, every now and then jabbing it upward. Once he almost left his seat like a streamer following the ascent of a kite. On the beach, T. G. had flown a kite and she'd liked that he was really into it, he wasn't trying to be cool. What happened, sometimes, that guys just stopped trying to impress you—or was even that a way of trying to impress? The man with the raised card won almost every lamp, and the auctioneer joked that "there'll be a hot time in the old town tonight!" "Las Vegas, Nevada!" some woman yelled, putting two fingers in her mouth and giving an earsplitting whistle. A child started to cry, and there was some shuffling of feet and concerned glances as its mother carried it outside. "So that does it for the King, the final curtain," the auctioneer said. "Iddn that right, boys? Happens to the best of us. Who were those boys in their glitter suits that their lion turned on one of 'em and he never worked again? That great, great act under the big top. We all remember that. Can't think you've made friends with a lion! And now we move on to the piece of resistance, as the Frenchies say. Some mighty fine courtin' might go on if you get yourself this furniture set, comfy cozy as a La-Z-Boy, and my boys are here to prove it. Sit yourself in that chair you're bringing up here, Donald, and tell us how comfy it feels. They don't make 'em like that anymore. Wheels on the legs, in case conversation gets borin' and you need to make a quick get-away! And who'll start us off at five hun-dred dollars?"

Bettina was riveted. Jocelyn was biting her bottom lip. Good god, was her aunt going to bid on it? No one was bidding. The set was already down to two hundred dollars. Jocelyn looked at Raleigh, who was looking at Bettina. He was clutching her hand so she didn't raise it. It was at one eighty. Bettina's card flew into the air. "Thank you kindly, and who gives one-ninety? One ninety? One ninety-five! Thank you, sir. At one ninety-five. Going once . . . thank you sir, two hundred. And two ten, yes, ma'am, lovely furniture—you got yourself a sweetheart, you plunk down on any of these pieces and it'll be a memorable evening . . . two twenty's the bid I'm looking for. Hold that chair up, Donald. I'm at two ten. Who'll make it two twenty? Real velvet upholstery. Going once, twice." The gavel came down.

Two hundred and ten dollars was the final bid, from someone behind them. Jocelyn's stomach turned over. It was Ms. Nementhal, she knew it. How could it not be? It was too perfect. Shit! Her aunt was craning her neck around to see who'd won it, but she'd never seen Ms. Nementhal, Raleigh had. Oh, please let me get out of here without having to speak to Ms. Nementhal, she prayed, and she didn't even believe in God, though what could you lose by saying a prayer? For weeks, she'd been thinking silent prayers. Her mother often talked about the Hand of Fate, which was even more ridiculous than believing in God.

A brass bed sold, and a chamber pot got a surprising number of bids. A birdcage with bird toys still in it went to the man in the wheelchair, who unlocked the chair's brakes and wheeled away to pay for it immediately. A floor lamp sold, its lightbulb still working. When the gavel came down for the last time, she turned to her aunt and said, "I don't feel so good. Can we leave?"

"I don't know why I let it get away," Bettina said. "It hardly went higher than the first bid. Why didn't I try harder?"

"You won't even remember it tomorrow," Raleigh said. "What would we do with furniture like that, Bettina?"

"I'll see you outside," Jocelyn said, forcing a smile and standing. It was true; she felt queasy. The smell of popcorn stung the air. They must be selling it at the concession stand. The salty smell was revolting. Okay, she could do it. Up and out. Head down. Ms. Nementhal would never know.

Except that Ms. Nementhal, bare feet in her clogs, arm linked with her girlfriend's (were they crazy to do that in a place like this?), looked up with her mouth full of popcorn as

Jocelyn walked by, and her eyes widened with such shock that it was clear her girlfriend was worried. Her girlfriend stood there holding the bag of popcorn, Ms. Nementhal's fingers searching inside, the half-naked doll in her other hand.

"Hi," Jocelyn said.

"Maura, this is one of my students," Ms. Nementhal said. "Some popcorn, Jocelyn?" She was trying to pretend everything was cool. Her girlfriend was extremely pretty, a lock of hair falling forward. She was holding the doll's arm as if it were a specimen of something she'd picked up with tweezers. Its messy, golden hair went in all directions. "Nice to meet you," her girlfriend said in a friendly way, with what might have been an Italian accent. Jocelyn exhaled and thought she might live through the moment.

"See you tomorrow," Jocelyn managed to say. She made it far enough away that she didn't think Ms. Nementhal saw her gag, though nothing came up.

What was it that made Jocelyn revise her essay that night? It could be fiction, so that was what she wrote, though she thought journalism was cool and fiction was sort of retarded. She wrote about someone who went to an auction with her husband, and they came home with (she couldn't do it; she couldn't say it was the doll) two Elvis lamps and had an argument about whose was better. The flash-forward part (which was required) was that five years later, when they were still arguing about the Elvis lamps, which they drove around in the backseat, they died in a car crash (please; enough of the Rapture!) and went to Heaven. God, who was sort of a joker, at first said he wouldn't let Elvis in, but then the lamps started singing and God relented, and decided which Elvis was better, then twerked with the winning Elvis like an actor at the end of a Bollywood movie. Jocelyn wrote the transition from the car crash to Heaven this way: "What they didn't know and wouldn't for some time was that they were dead, and that meant they could have what they wanted. Not what they feared . . . not what they said silent prayers hoping to ward off . . . but anything they wanted." Jocelyn wasn't sure about the three dots for punctuation, whatever they were called, but she'd tried a colon first and that didn't look right. She continued: "So they decided on Heaven and before they blinked they'd arrived though it took them years to realize it because time goes very slowly there, and God did not at first appear." She knew the last comma was correct because it was a compound sentence joined by the word *and*. It got her a B.

Here's what the Hand of Fate wrote: Jocelyn had to go forward, she couldn't look back. Not even at the indentation in the sand where they'd had sex. The sand wouldn't look different, and if you bothered to turn around and look, who wouldn't want what met their eye to be worthy of their hesitation, their double take, special? Sand was ordinary. So was the face of her friend Zelda, who'd shown up that night, running down the beach, trailing her scarf, sensing something was up. She and T. G. never talked about having sex that one time. He wasn't her first. Not long afterward, he tried to kill himself, though the two things were unrelated. She went to an auction with her aunt and uncle when she was seven weeks pregnant. The auction was a sad affair, and all the time she sat there, she had a feeling that she knew what was wrong. Not just what was wrong with her but what was wrong all around her, with people bantering and wasting time, sitting passively

ABOUT THE AUTHOR

Ann Beattie has been included in four O. Henry Award collections, in John Updike's *The Best American Short Stories of the Century*, and in Jennifer Egan's *The Best American Short Stories 2014*. In 2000, she received the PEN/Malamud Award for achievement in the short story. In 2005, she received the Rea Award for the Short Story. She was the Edgar Allan Poe Professor of Literature and Creative Writing at the University of Virginia. She is a member of the American Academy of Arts and Letters and of the American Academy of Arts and Sciences. She and her husband, Lincoln Perry, live in Maine and Key West, Florida.